On Sunday Benjamin Passmore opened his eyes to darkness, as he had every morning for the past few years. For several minutes he lay in bed staring into the dark shapelessness that was all he ever saw now. From the kitchen, he heard the distinct sounds of his mother opening and closing cabinets, followed by a "damn" as she dropped a large pot on the floor.

It was hard to believe that in less than two weeks, on December twenty-seventh, he would go under the knife at Boston General Hospital. Benjamin would be a glorified guinea pig for experimental laser surgery that doctors hoped would restore his sight.

Benjamin rolled over, burying his head under his pillow. Every time he contemplated the idea of being able to see again, his heart rate speeded up to about two hundred beats a minute. Mostly the prospect of opening his eyes to a bright, colorful world every morning exhilarated him. But in those moments of clear and unguarded reflection, Benjamin admitted that he was terrified.

Don't miss any of the books in
Making Out
*by Katherine Applegate
from Avon Flare*

#1 ZOEY FOOLS AROUND
#2 JAKE FINDS OUT
#3 NINA WON'T TELL
#4 BEN'S IN LOVE
#5 CLAIRE GETS CAUGHT
#6 WHAT ZOEY SAW
#7 LUCAS GETS HURT
#8 AISHA GOES WILD
#9 ZOEY PLAYS GAMES
#10 NINA SHAPES UP
#11 BEN TAKES A CHANCE

Coming Soon

#12 CLAIRE CAN'T LOSE

Ben
takes
a chance

KATHERINE APPLEGATE

AN AVON FLARE BOOK

AVON BOOKS, INC.
1350 Avenue of the Americas
New York, New York 10019

Copyright © 1996 by Daniel Weiss Associates, Inc., and
Katherine Applegate
Published by arrangement with Daniel Weiss Associates, Inc.
Library of Congress Catalog Card Number: 98-93666
ISBN: 0-380-80867-6
www.avonbooks.com/chathamisland

First Avon Flare Printing: April 1999

AVON FLARE TRADEMARK REG. U.S. PAT. OFF. AND IN OTHER COUNTRIES, MARCA REGISTRADA, HECHO EN U.S.A.

Printed in the U.S.A.

WCD   10   9   8   7   6   5   4   3   2   1

Ben takes a chance

Zoey

Sex? Sometimes when I hear that word I feel like screaming. I spend half my time keeping Lucas's mind away from that territory. But it's hard, especially considering that sex is everywhere you look. I mean, I think they're using scantily clad women to sell floor wax these days.

To be totally and completely honest, I'm pretty ignorant in the sex department. Not that my mom hasn't tried to approach the dreaded subject on several occasions. But I tell her I learned everything I needed to know about the topic from _Our Bodies, Ourselves_ and Judy Blume's _Forever_.

1

Anything else, I guess
I'll discover on my own.
Someday.

All of this talk about sex
leads me to another big
issue in my life right now:
Lucas versus Aaron.
Whereas Lucas is in a
huge hurry to have sex,
Aaron doesn't even believe
in sex before marriage. I
like that about him.

Because the truth is,
having sex symbolizes
something for me. It means
growing up and worrying
about consequences. And
right now the only
consequences I want to
consider are how the
calories in a pint of Ben &
Jerry's are going to affect
the size of my hips and
butt.

Does that make any sense?
Like, at all?

LUCAS

I want to have sex with Zoey very, very badly. I think about it every day, every hour, every minute. The only time I don't think about it is when I'm talking to my mother. In general, mothers are a great cure for horniness.

But if I can't have sex with Zoey, I want to do it with someone else. Someone beautiful, I hope. And experienced.

I wouldn't have written that down if you'd asked me yesterday. But yesterday is over. And right now I'm not sure if there's any point in waiting it out with Zoey.

3

Aisha

I've had sex. This information is what I call classified. A few select people are aware of this fact (ie, Zoey and Nina), but Christopher has no idea.

You might say to me, "Aisha, you dishonest scum bucket. You're letting your boyfriend believe you're a virgin, when in fact you've already done it with another guy."

But the fact that I've had sex in the past doesn't mean I want to now. We women try to learn from our mistakes, unlike the inferior, stupider half of our species.

I thought I was pregnant once, back when I lived in Boston. The days before the test came up negative were without a doubt the worst in my life. Have you ever stood at the edge of a steep, rocky cliff? You know that if you take even one tiny step, you'll be falling into a deep, dark abyss. That's what thinking I

4

was pregnant felt like. I didn't think I'd ever be so happy to need a tampon. But I'm telling you, seeing that telltale spot of blood on my underwear was better than sex could ever be.

Let's face it. The guy tells you he loves you. He might even mean it. But when the baby shows up, screaming and pooping and needing braces and a college education, he's out the door.

Sex does strange things to people. Crazy, irrational things. And I like to have my wits about me, especially when my entire future is at stake.

Christopher

I LOVE SEX. I LOVE EVERYTHING ABOUT IT. UNFORTUNATELY, IT'S BEEN A REALLY LONG TIME SINCE I'VE HAD ANYTHING CLOSE TO SEX, SO I'M TALKING FROM MEMORY HERE.

OF COURSE, AISHA'S WORTH BEING PATIENT FOR. SHE'S STILL A VIRGIN, SO I KNOW WE HAVE TO TAKE THINGS SLOWLY. THERE'S A LOT OF PASSION BEHIND HER COOL BROWN EYES. IT'S JUST A MATTER OF WAITING TILL THE TIME IS RIGHT.

One

On Sunday nineteen-year-old Benjamin Passmore opened his eyes to darkness, as he had every morning for the past few years. For several minutes he lay in bed staring into the dark shapelessness that was all he ever saw now. From the kitchen, he heard the distinct sounds of his mother opening and closing cabinets, followed by a "damn" as she dropped a large pot on the floor.

Benjamin sighed as he automatically reached for the small Braille clock he kept by his bed. It was either 9:01 or 9:02 A.M., and already he was wide awake. He usually slept late on Sunday mornings, but he knew he'd never be able to drift back to la-la land. Too many worries were crowding his brain.

It was hard to believe that in less than two weeks, on December twenty-seventh, he would go under the knife at Boston General Hospital. Benjamin would be a glorified guinea pig for experimental laser surgery that doctors hoped would restore his sight.

Benjamin rolled over, burying his head under his pillow. Every time he contemplated the idea of being able to see again, his heart rate speeded up to about two hundred beats a minute. Mostly the prospect of opening his eyes to a bright, colorful world every morning exhilarated him. But in those moments of clear and unguarded reflection, Benjamin admitted to himself that he was terrified.

Since the possibility of surgery had emerged, he'd had more arguments with his girlfriend, Nina Geiger, than he cared to contemplate. Just the day before, she'd practically thrown him out of her house when he'd suggested that she should spend New Year's Eve with all of their friends on Chatham Island rather than reading back issues of *People* in his Boston hospital room.

For the first time since he'd woken up, Benjamin grinned. He and Nina had also been closer, both literally and figuratively, since the whole issue of the operation had surfaced. After years of cold showers and frustrating dreams, Benjamin had lost his virginity in the not-so-regal splendor of the Malibu Hotel in Boston. That was another event he'd anticipated with both exhilaration and terror.

"Benjamin!" Darla Passmore called from outside his bedroom door. "Are you awake?"

Benjamin reached for his Ray-Bans. "Yeah, Mom."

"I've got a plate of pancakes for you. They're at your usual seat. Syrup's at three o'clock."

"Thanks," he called back.

"I'm going to go get your sister." He listened to her footsteps fade down the hallway, and he adjusted his glasses.

For a moment Benjamin allowed himself to imagine a life in which his mother wouldn't have to inform him about the whereabouts of the maple syrup. A wave of images from his childhood flooded over him: playing basketball with his dad at the playground while Zoey ran to the swing set; seeing how the wind pulled at Zoey's wispy hair and tore through the treetops. As a child he had wanted, in rapid succession, to be a police officer, a firefighter, and a veterinarian. Until he'd lost his sight, he'd never really had to think about whether he'd be able to make such dreams and expectations come true; he'd just assumed that anything was possible. Could that kind of freedom to imagine the future—a future unlimited by his blindness—be restored to him?

Fantasizing too much was dangerous. He had gotten through the loss of his eyesight once, only because he hadn't fully understood how painful it would be. But knowing what he did now, could he endure losing everything a second time?

Benjamin swung his feet over the side of the bed, wincing when the cold air hit his bare legs. December twenty-seventh. There was no turning back now.

Zoey Passmore tried very hard not to wake up on Sunday morning. The first glimmer of consciousness hit her in the stomach. The feeling was somewhere between seasickness and a jab from Mike Tyson. She rolled over, crushed a pillow against her head, and tried to convince herself that she was in fact still sleeping. Unfortunately, the sound of her mother moving around the kitchen and the ringing of the telephone didn't quite fit into her dream (in which she'd been magically reincarnated as Mary Poppins).

Zoey groaned, resigned to the fact that the memory of the worst night of her life was about to hit like a tidal wave. She curled into a fetal position, bracing herself.

Her strict code of love and morality had not been strong enough to hold up to forbidden fruit. She'd succumbed to her weaker self. In other words, Zoey had made out with Aaron again.

And she'd hurt Lucas. The image of his face as he burst into the room and caught them together kept playing over and over in Zoey's mind. His longish blond hair had been in appealing disarray, while his dark eyes had stared at her in horror. Still breathing heavily from Aaron's kisses, Zoey had realized that Lucas really was the guy she loved—more than anything. She had blown it.

Sunlight streamed into her windows. Shrouding herself in her down comforter and squinting to keep the light out of her eyes, Zoey shuffled across her hardwood floor and pulled down her shades. She would put Bonnie Raitt's song "Guilty" on repeat play, get back in bed, and wallow in self-recrimination. Maybe by the next day she could manage to rediscover the muscles in her neck and actually hold up her head.

There was a soft rapping at her door. Zoey's heart leaped. The previous evening had been a nightmare, a horrible nightmare that was now over. Lucas was at her door to apologize, and they were going to roll around on her bed and discuss how much they loved each other.

"Zoey, it's me." The door opened a crack.

"Oh, hi, Mom," Zoey whispered, struggling to keep the disappointment out of her voice.

Darla Passmore opened the door wider and stuck her head inside. "I'm making pancakes. Come downstairs."

Zoey shook her head. "I'm not really hungry." *I'm not even sure I'm still breathing*, she added silently.

Mrs. Passmore crossed the room and opened

10

Zoey's shades with two quick flicks of her wrist. "Zo, how often does your no-good mom make a big family breakfast? You've got to seize the day and stuff yourself with pancakes and maple syrup."

Zoey sank onto her bed. If she refused to go downstairs, her mom would probably try to engage her in some heavy-duty, heart-to-heart, mother-daughter tell-all. And Zoey was definitely not in the mood to spill her miserable guts.

"Okay, I'll be down in a minute."

Mrs. Passmore ran a gentle hand over Zoey's hair. "Great, hon. I'll make up a plate for you."

After Mrs. Passmore was gone, Zoey opened the bottom drawer of her bureau, where she kept all of her clothes that weren't fit to be seen in public. She pulled out her grungiest sweatpants and a hole-ridden sweater that had belonged to her father during his Woodstock days.

Taking off the maroon Boston Bruins nightshirt she always wore to bed seemed like too great an effort on the worst morning of her life. Instead, Zoey stuffed the tail of the shirt into her sweatpants, then pulled on the orange sweater. She started to pick up her brush but left her hand suspended in midair.

Grooming was a thing that happy, normal people did. She was the scum of the earth, a low-down piece of gum stuck on the shoe of humanity. She didn't care that her long dark blond hair was a collection of tangles. She didn't even care that there was still sleep in the corners of her blue eyes. She felt horrible, and she wanted her appearance to match.

Downstairs, Benjamin was cutting up his pancakes into neat squares with his fork and knife. "Morning, Zo," he said blandly.

"Yeah, whatever." Zoey examined Benjamin's

face, searching for signs that he knew what had taken place in her bedroom the night before. His expression was decidedly neutral, which led Zoey to believe that he knew everything.

"Go get Lara, will you?" Mrs. Passmore said from the other side of the kitchen, where she was pouring pancake batter onto a griddle.

Zoey rolled her eyes. "Why not?" The day couldn't get any worse. Maybe Lara's dismal presence would distract her from the fact that she'd ruined her life.

Zoey walked toward the front door, dimly aware that her head felt like a huge, cumbersome bowling ball. As far as Zoey was concerned, her world would be a little more bearable if her half sister, Lara McAvoy, had never shown up on the family's doorstep.

The girl was rude, weird, and a major pain in the ass. Shortly after Thanksgiving she'd moved into the room above the Passmores' garage. Since then, she'd managed to slither her way into the life of Zoey's ex-boyfriend, Jake McRoyan.

Zoey shivered as she ran from the house to the steps that led to Lara's room. Despite the sunshine, the temperature of the mid-December air hovered somewhere around thirty degrees. Zoey knocked loudly on the door. "Lara!"

There was no answer. Zoey knocked again. "Lara, my mom made pancakes."

Zoey heard nothing. Not even an irritated groan or the sound of a pillow being hurled against the door. Apparently Lara was a heavy sleeper. Of course, Zoey had recently learned from Jake that Lara liked to drink herself to sleep every night. From what Zoey understood, alcohol was great for inducing unconsciousness.

Slowly Zoey opened the door of Lara's room. "Lara?" she called again.

The room was empty. Lara's bed was unmade. But now that she thought of it, Zoey had never seen Lara's bed anywhere close to being made. On a small table in the corner of the room, a lamp was switched on. Zoey raised her eyebrows. Why would someone turn on a light on a sunny morning? Obviously the lamp had been left on all night.

Back in the kitchen, Benjamin appeared to be on his second plate of pancakes. "She's not there," Zoey announced.

Mrs. Passmore turned away from the stove. "What do you mean?"

Zoey shrugged. "Lara's not in her room. I don't think she's been there all night."

"Where could she possibly be?" Mrs. Passmore asked, frowning.

"How should I know?" Zoey sat down at the kitchen table.

Benjamin was mushing a piece of pancake through his syrup absently. He didn't look up as Zoey took her usual seat and stabbed a fork into the pancakes on her plate.

Poor Jake. Zoey had a feeling that Lara made every guy she touched miserable. Then again, Zoey'd been doing a pretty good job of that herself lately. She had hurt her boyfriend, had led Aaron on. And her brother looked as though he were going to his own execution, though that wasn't Zoey's doing.

Zoey put a hand on Benjamin's arm. "How're you doing?" she asked him.

"Better than you, I think." He grinned wryly.

JAKE

What I wish I could say is that the first time I had sex was this incredible, awesome, unforgettable experience. But that would be a lie. I don't remember losing my virginity. I wouldn't even know I had, except that the girl I did it with, Louise Kronenberger, told me about it later. I was wasted out of my mind at the time. The only clear image I have of the experience is a portion of Louise's very smooth, very firm thigh. Other than that, it's a total blank.

Claire

I've never had sex, although I like to let on that maybe I have. Mystery is a good tool.

I'm simply not an intimate person. Life is a lot less painful if you keep people (even people you love) at a distance. At least I think that's why I'm still a virgin, since God knows I've had plenty of opportunities to do It.

Then again, I have to face the fact that there may be some moral core inside of me. A little voice says you should actually be married before the big event.

I suppose that voice might belong to my mother. It's possible that she instilled some of those good old family values in us Geiger girls before she died.

Two

Jake McRoyan was vaguely aware that his head was resting on a very soft pillow. He moved his head from side to side, savoring the last few minutes of sleep. A moment later he realized that moving his head, or any part of his body, was not a good idea. His body felt as if it had been run through a juicer.

Jake concentrated all of his effort on opening his eyes. He jerked away from Lara McAvoy immediately. What was she doing sleeping in his bed? Jake lifted the edge of his comforter and peered beneath. What was she doing *naked* in his bed?

Jake's eyes suddenly popped wide open. The whole night—most of the night, at least—came rushing back to him. Lara had come over while he was trying to write his way overdue paper on *The Scarlet Letter*. She'd had a bottle of Jack Daniels, and she'd somehow convinced Jake that it was a good idea for him to bag his English paper, along with his newfound clean and sober lifestyle, and get drunk with her. After the bottle was gone, Jake had sneaked upstairs and taken another from his father's liquor cabinet. Then they'd fallen into bed. . . .

Lara moved against him, then opened the blue eyes that reminded him so much of Zoey's. "Good morning, Jake," she said softly. Her breath had the sickly sweet smell that Jake recognized from his own past drinking binges.

He started to pull away, but Lara pulled him close. Her tangled dirty-blond hair brushed against his chest. "Kiss me."

Jake closed his eyes, wishing away the hangover that was making its presence known in his head, his arms, his legs, and—worst of all—his stomach. Lara's lips were soft and teasing, but for possibly the first time in his post-puberty life, Jake had no desire to fool around. He pulled away, embarrassed.

"Lara, about last night . . ."

She stretched, allowing the comforter to slip down to her waist. "Wasn't it great?"

Jake cleared his throat, wondering how to respond. "Uh, yeah."

Parts of the night *had* been great. And Lara's wide blue eyes seemed to be begging him to say something nice. Jake had never before woken up with a girl beside him in bed, but instinct told him that informing said girl the whole thing had been a huge mistake was *not* a good idea.

Before he had a chance to pay an appropriate compliment, there was a loud knock on his bedroom door. "Jake! Wake up," Mrs. McRoyan called. "Time to get ready for church."

A wave of panic surged through his body, momentarily overpowering the effects of his hangover. He threw the comforter over Lara's head. "Uh, okay, Mom. I'll get up right now."

Under the comforter, Lara began giggling. She also started to tickle Jake, who felt that disaster was imminent. "Is everything all right in there?" Mrs. McRoyan asked.

"Fine!" Jake squeaked. "I just, uh, hit my funny bone . . . but it's okay now."

As soon as Mrs. McRoyan's footsteps faded down the hallway, Lara popped up from under the covers. "Close call, Jake. Mommy almost found you with your hand in the cookie jar."

Jake sank back into his pillows. The idea of going to church was about as appealing as a wake-up shot of Jack Daniels, but he didn't have much choice. Since Jake's older brother, Wade, had died in a drunk driving accident two years earlier, Mrs. McRoyan had become a devout church-goer. As her only surviving child, Jake felt it was his duty to accompany her whenever humanly possible.

"We shouldn't have gotten drunk last night, Lara," he said softly.

She frowned. "Don't you like being with me?"

Jake grabbed a dirty towel from a chair next to his bed. "You know that's not the point." He stood up, quickly wrapping the towel around his waist.

Still lounging in the bed, Lara looked amused. "What *is* the point?"

Jake sat back down, careful not to make contact with any distracting sections of Lara's flesh. "I don't know what the point is, except that . . ."

"Except what, Jake?" She traced the line of his forearm with her fingers, then moved to put her head in his lap.

"We made a promise to each other last night," he said finally.

"We did?" she asked, her voice laced with exaggerated innocence.

"Yep. We vowed that neither one of us was ever going to drink again." He paused. "Last night was it. End of story."

18

"Oh, that promise. Sure, Jake. I remember."

Jake felt a sinking sensation in his stomach that had nothing to do with dehydration or alcohol poisoning. Over the last few weeks he'd learned that Lara didn't always keep her promises. What was going to happen the next time she approached him with a bottle of Jack Daniels? Or a flask of tequila? Or a twelve-pack of Budweiser?

Would he have the strength to say no?

Three

"Aisha, telephone." Carol Gray held the phone out to her daughter, who was sitting at the breakfast table.

Aisha jumped up, sending her silverware clattering to the floor. Just as abruptly, she sat back down. "I'm not here. Okay, Mom?"

"Is something wrong, Aisha?"

Aisha Gray blinked rapidly, realizing that her parents and her little brother, Kalif, were all watching her around the table. "No, no. Everything's fine. Great. Wonderful. I just want to enjoy a peaceful meal with my family."

Aisha saw Mrs. Gray raise an eyebrow in the direction of her husband. "Are you sure? It's Christopher."

Aisha put on her brightest smile. If any of them got wind of what was going on, she'd never have the calm, peaceful environment necessary to make the biggest decision of her entire life.

"Positive." To avoid her mother's penetrating gaze, she picked up her coffee cup and took a large swallow. Then she gagged.

Kalif snorted, and Alan Gray remained characteristically silent. Mrs. Gray hung up the phone and returned to the table. "Aisha, you put sugar on your waffles and syrup in your coffee," Mrs. Gray pointed out.

Aisha glanced down at her waffles, then felt her stomach do a flip-flop. She was obviously in no condition to be around other human beings. Especially when those humans happened to be members of her family.

"I think I'll take a shower," she announced. Without waiting for a response, Aisha bolted from her chair.

"Don't forget that we've got to change all of the flowers later," Mrs. Gray called.

Aisha nodded, then breathed a sigh of relief as she stepped beyond the kitchen door.

The Grays lived at Gray House, an old inn her parents had bought and renovated into a bed-and-breakfast a few years earlier, when they'd moved to Chatham Island.

Christopher Shupe, Aisha's boyfriend, had shown up on Chatham Island only a few months ago. Having graduated from high school in the inner city, he'd decided to move to Maine to earn money for college. He'd immediately gotten himself at least three jobs, one of which was helping Mrs. Gray with yard work. Unfortunately, the onset of winter had cost him a lot of his income. Now he was down to his job as a cook at Passmores', the restaurant Zoey's parents owned, and delivering papers in the morning. Which was why he needed money. Which was why—

Aisha's thoughts broke off as she saw Sarah and Aaron Mendel walking toward the front door.

"Good morning, Aisha!" Mrs. Mendel called.

"Uh, good morning." Aisha looked down at her

tattered robe and slippers. Her mom wouldn't appreciate having a guest see her like that. She sprinted toward her bedroom.

Usually Gray House was free of guests by December. The peak tourist season lasted from June through August, and after that the Grays would gradually reclaim their home from guests. But that year Burke Geiger's new girlfriend, Sarah Mendel, and her son, Aaron, were spending several weeks at the quaint B&B.

As Aisha opened the door of her first-floor bedroom, she pondered the fact that the rest of Chatham Island seemed to be carrying on as if nothing monumental had happened. As if her whole world hadn't been completely turned inside out in the last twenty-four hours.

Of course, she reminded herself, as of yet nobody but she and Christopher were aware of what had taken place at exactly 9:28 the night before.

Aisha flopped on her bed, clutching her oldest teddy bear tightly to her chest. Had the previous night even been real? Maybe the whole evening had been one of those superrealistic dreams she'd heard about on *Unsolved Mysteries*. Maybe the whole time she *thought* she'd been with Christopher she'd actually been snoring and drooling in her bed.

Aisha rolled over to get a view of the closet door. The black strapless dress her mother had loaned Aisha for her date with Christopher was hanging on the back of the door. Check. Below it were the high-heeled black pumps she wore for virtually every occasion that called for a skirt. Another check. Then she leaned over and pulled open the drawer of her nightstand. The pack of matches she'd taken from the restaurant the previous night was nestled among old play programs, movie stubs, and lift tickets from the gang's recent ski trip to Vermont. Check.

Aisha needed only one more piece of evidence to confirm that her Saturday night had definitely not been part of a dream. She threw the teddy bear against her poster of Queen Latifah and heaved herself from the bed.

Feeling like a zombie, Aisha moved slowly toward the oak bureau that stood next to her closet. She opened the bottom drawer, inch by inch, until she was staring at a collection of wool sweaters and ragged turtlenecks. The tips of her fingers tingling, she took a deep breath and plunged her hand to the bottom of the drawer. It took only a second to locate the tiny velvet box.

Aisha's heart pounded as she closed her fist around the box. It was really true. Christopher had asked her to marry him. He wanted her to be his wife. Forever.

Walking back to her bed, Aisha held the box as if it were a ticking bomb. She glanced at the door to make sure it was firmly shut before she allowed herself to look at the antique silver ring.

Careful not to crush the delicate velvet that surrounded the ring, Aisha lifted it from the tiny cushion. Her breath caught in her throat as she studied the simple band. Whether or not to wear that ring was the biggest decision Aisha had ever had to make. Aisha gripped the ring tightly as she forced herself to think about the other thing Christopher had told her.

After she'd finished her pasta, Christopher had informed her that he'd decided to join the United States Army. All Aisha had been able to do in response to that news was shake her head. Just thinking about those few minutes, when her world had seemed to be on the verge of utter collapse, made Aisha feel short of breath.

Through her tears, she'd seen Christopher's chocolate brown eyes gazing into hers. When he'd asked her to marry him, another choking fit had brought over three waiters and the maître d'. The whole episode had ended with free dessert and coffee for Christopher and Aisha.

But all through the creme caramel, then the water taxi ride back to the island, the question had lingered between them. Aisha was only seventeen years old, Christopher only nineteen. They could each easily live another seventy or eighty years. And committing herself to eighty years of *anything* was a daunting prospect. She just hadn't been able to bring herself to say yes. Then again, she hadn't been able to say no, either.

Aisha slipped the ring over her left ring finger. She held her hand away from her face, noting how the smooth silver gleamed brightly against her dark skin. Aisha gulped. She felt as if she never wanted to take the band off.

Claire Geiger stood at the edge of the widow's walk above her room, shivering slightly inside the Patagonia jacket she'd pulled on over her thin nightgown. Thick gray clouds were hanging low in the sky. Claire predicted rain, possibly snow, by late afternoon. She made a mental note to monitor the temperature as the day passed.

For many years Claire had been fascinated by weather patterns. Every morning she checked the barometer mounted on the wall next to the trapdoor that led to the widow's walk, then scanned the sky and the ocean for signs of storms. She planned to study in Antarctica someday, where weather was at its most severe.

Lately Claire had a new hobby. His name was Aaron Mendel, and he was the first guy Claire had met in a long time whom she thought she might actually be able to fall in love with.

Turning to look down the street in front of the Geigers' home, Claire smiled smugly. In less than an hour Aaron and his mother would be walking down that street, heading straight for Claire's front door.

Claire idly twisted a strand of her long black hair as her thoughts drifted to the events of the past few weeks. Who would have thought that her dad's finding a girlfriend might serve as a conduit for Claire herself to find true love? When she'd heard that Sarah Mendel was bringing her son to Thanksgiving dinner, Claire had not expected to find him incredibly handsome and intelligent.

But Claire had known almost immediately that Aaron was a kindred spirit. He'd fooled the rest of Chatham Island (especially Zoey) with his charming smile and Victorian-gentleman manners, but Claire saw beneath the facade. She'd recognized herself in him: the ability to manipulate, the frustration with banal people, the desire to be in control. Those were qualities Claire admired, and Aaron possessed every single one.

But so far Aaron hadn't made the conquest easy for her. He'd gone straight for Zoey. And Zoey was too naive to see that once he'd made her fall madly in love with him, Aaron would leave her out in the street for the Monday morning garbage pickup.

Poor, poor Zoey. She was lucky that Claire had

finally taken mercy on her (in a you've-got-to-be-cruel-to-be-kind sort of way) and started implementing her plan to bring Zoey's life back to dull normalcy.

Despite herself, Claire felt a twinge of guilt. While *Claire* was certain that calling Lucas on Saturday night and informing him that Aaron was at Zoey's house had been the right thing to do, she was sure Lucas had gotten quite a shock.

But Claire knew from experience that when people weren't behaving in the way that was best for them—or for her—she had to take matters into her own hands. And that was exactly what she'd done.

Claire started walking toward the ladder that led to her room. She wanted to look her best for brunch. Aaron was finally going to see that Zoey was more trouble than she was worth.

For the first time since she'd discovered the Red Hot Chili Peppers, Nina Geiger had no desire to listen to music. Her head was so crowded with disturbing thoughts that she felt adding the boom of a bass rhythm might truly drive her insane.

Nina stood uncertainly in the middle of her room. She'd gotten out of the shower a full five minutes before, but she'd made no move to get dressed. Instead, she clutched the towel wrapped around her torso and watched drop after drop of water fall from her hair to the small throw rug she was standing on.

Feeling like an idiot, she finally let the towel fall to the floor. With reluctance, she moved to stand in front of the full-length mirror that was attached to the inside of her closet door. For days she'd been wondering if losing her virginity had had an overall impact on her appearance.

But Nina didn't make a habit of studying her nude body. In gym class she was always the girl who tried to change at lightning speed and with her breasts facing a row of lockers. She'd made something of an art out of learning to expose the least amount of flesh possible at any given moment.

Whenever she did get the urge to check herself out in the privacy of her room, she had the terrifying sense that someone was going to pop out from the shadows and scream, "Surprise! You're on *Candid Camera*!" Then the video of her naked body would end up on *Hard Copy*, and she'd never be able to leave the house again.

But now Nina stared at her fresh-from-the-shower body with great interest. She'd had sex for the first time several days earlier. Shouldn't she be blossoming into true womanhood by now? The romances Zoey always read talked about "rosy glows."

As far as Nina could tell, she had no rosy glow. Her breasts were still on the very small side, and her hips and legs looked as unremarkable as they had in the past. As usual, her dark hair was sticking out in all directions. She wondered, as she often did, how it was possible for one sister to be a Brooke Shields look-alike while the other was just plain . . . average.

Nina moved her face close to the mirror, staring intently into her own eyes. Was there a deeper understanding there? Had a secret been unlocked from her soul? She shook her head. They were the same dull shade of gray they'd been forever.

Benjamin had seemed pleased enough with her various body parts in the past, but he was blind. If he got his sight back after the operation, he might realize how attractive he was and decide to let Nina eat dust. She could already imagine the conversation.

"Nina, you're a great girl," he would say. "But I think we should be just friends. . . ."

Nina turned abruptly from the mirror. Still naked, she rummaged through her top desk drawer until she found a nearly empty pack of Lucky Strikes. She took out one of the three remaining cigarettes and popped it in her mouth. As always, Nina felt calmed by the act of sucking on the unlit Lucky Strike. It was a habit her friends (and the school administration) found unnerving, but Nina felt she needed a vice. And as far as she knew, puffing on unlit cigarettes posed no serious health threat.

She lay down on her unmade bed, conscious of the unfamiliar sensation of her bare flesh against the sheets.

"Nina, are you in there?" Claire yelled, banging on Nina's dead-bolted bedroom door.

Irrationally, Nina dove under her covers. Unless Claire had either X-ray vision or was carrying a heavy-duty crowbar, there was no way she'd find out Nina was lounging in bed au naturel.

"What do you want?" Nina yelled.

"Miss Sunshine and her offspring will be here any minute. You'd better get your butt downstairs."

As usual, Claire didn't bother with polite good-byes. Nina heard her older sister take off down the hall before she had a chance to make a rude comment. Nina frowned. She hated to miss an opportunity to insult Princess Claire.

Groaning, Nina dragged herself off the bed. She'd forgotten that her dad had scheduled yet another tedious get-together with his new girlfriend (if a woman over forty could still be referred to as a *girl*). By Nina's estimation, Burke Geiger had regressed approximately thirty years since meeting

Sarah at the bank he owned in Weymouth.

Nina pulled out a tattered pair of cotton underwear and some faded Levi's. She was anxious to get back to her natural state, which was clothed. Pulling on a plaid flannel shirt, Nina chided herself for the hundredth time since her father had started his relationship with Sarah.

For months Nina had been worried about the possibility of her father ending up a lonely old man. Nina's mother had died five years before, and since then Mr. Geiger hadn't had so much as dinner and a cognac with another woman. But now that he was actually entering the land of the living, Nina felt defensive. Sarah Mendel was nothing like her mother had been.

While Mrs. Geiger had been cool and elegant, Mrs. Mendel resembled one of the Munchkins from *The Wizard of Oz*. She was petite and perky, and her smile seemed sewn into place. Basically, she was the exact opposite of Nina, who hadn't come close to resembling perky since she was three years old.

Nina yanked a brush through a knot in her hair. She had a suspicion that Claire was attracted to Sarah's son, Aaron, although she treated him with the same superior indifference that she used on everybody else. Nina would have to watch Claire carefully during brunch. Maybe she'd learn something interesting. Something that would distract her from thinking about Benjamin's surgery, which was only twelve days away.

Nina

Sex? Sex, sex, sex. If you'd asked me about the dirty deed a few weeks ago, I would've been, like, huh? I mean, back then the extent of my sexual knowledge came straight from _Forever_ by Judy Blume. Like, I knew that sex could get you pregnant, which would lead to either (a) an abortion, (b) a horrible adoption that would someday become a primetime miniseries, or (c) keeping the kid and leaving adolescence far behind (not necessarily such a bad thing). I also knew sex could kill you if you had it with a guy who'd had the really bad luck to get AIDS from his high-school sweetheart, who he'd thought was a virgin.

In other words, my feelings about sex were purely analytical. You know, where everybody's equipment goes, what happens (more or less), and all of the evil that could result from the act. But several weeks ago I was a virgin. (That word seems like it should be capitalized.)

Now I'm not. Benjamin and I had sex when we went to Boston together. What can I say about it? Jeez. A lot. I could probably write a whole book about the experience. First of all, it was weird. And nice. Really nice.

You'd think sex with a blind guy would be a particular challenge. But the fact is, people usually have sex in the dark anyway, so what's the difference?

We were both really nervous. The matter of getting the condom on him would be a whole chapter in itself. And it was Benjamin's first time, too, so I think he was ultra-aware of his impending status as a man, in every sense of the word.

I was pretty relieved when the whole ordeal was over, to tell you the truth. Not that I didn't like it. I loved it. I think I loved it.

BENJAMIN

I think sex takes on special importance for a blind person. Not being able to see makes me particularly aware of the other senses—like touch.

Having sex with Nina was the most incredible thing I've ever experienced. Afterward, I felt so close to her that I wished I could just take her whole being and fuse it with mine.

I mean, I knew I was in love with Nina before the actual act. But there'd always been a barrier—my blindness. No matter what was going on, I knew Nina was experiencing things I couldn't even imagine: looking at a poster, checking her watch, noticing a zit on my face.

But when we were making love, I felt like we were really together. It was as though my blindness disappeared in the tangle of arms and legs and mouths. The word that comes to mind is *beautiful*.

I just hope it was as good for Nina.

Four

Sunday evening Lucas Cabral switched off the television set when Andy Rooney's face appeared on the screen. He'd never understood why *60 Minutes* kept that guy under contract. He worked for only a couple of minutes a week, and he still managed to be the most annoying TV personality in the United States.

Without the sound of the television, the Cabrals' living room was deadly quiet. Mr. Cabral was already asleep; as a lobsterman, he had to rise at four in the morning to take out his boat. In the kitchen, Lucas's mother was washing the dinner dishes and quietly humming Christmas hymns to herself.

Lucas stared at the Christmas tree his father had put up in a corner of the room. Despite its white lights and colorful ornaments, the sight of the tree deepened Lucas's depression. He'd spent the last two Christmases in Youth Authority, where he'd been sent after falsely confessing that he'd been driving drunk the night Wade McRoyan had been killed in a car accident. In fact, Claire (whom Lucas had been in love with at the time) had been driving.

As much as he claimed to hate holidays, Lucas had secretly been looking forward to this Christmas.

He'd imagined sitting by the fireplace at the Passmores', exchanging presents and kisses (maybe even more than kisses) with Zoey. Now he had every reason to believe that he'd spend December twenty-fifth sitting in awkward silence with his parents, who happened to be two of the least cheerful people he'd ever met.

Sighing, Lucas crossed the living room toward the tree. He knelt down and pulled the plug of the strand of lights from the electrical outlet behind the tree.

Finally Lucas caved in to the urge he'd been resisting all day. He stepped out onto the small deck behind the house. From there he could see the back of the Passmores' house. On most mornings he'd stand at the edge of the deck and gaze into Zoey's kitchen. When she finally rushed to the breakfast table, he'd feel that his morning had really begun.

Now the kitchen was dark, echoing Lucas's mood. As he stared at the house, he longed to jump the deck railing and sprint the short distance to the other house. But he couldn't. It was possible that even at that very moment Aaron Mendel was in Zoey's bedroom. The idea made Lucas want to throw up.

Swallowing hard, he forced himself to turn from the Passmores'. Even if he couldn't seek refuge at Zoey's, he had to get out of his own house. The suffocating silence that allowed him to be alone with his thoughts would drive him mad before the night was over.

If nothing else, he could swim out to sea and drown himself. Maybe then Zoey would be sorry.

As soon as he heard the knock on his door, Christopher Shupe tossed aside the army pamphlets he'd been reading. He looked quickly into the small mirror on his wall, grinning at himself.

Aisha had kept him in suspense for almost twenty-four hours, and now she was finally going to say yes to his proposal. Thank goodness the waiting was over. He understood that women liked to play hard to get, but there was only so much a man could take. As he moved to the door, Christopher wondered if Aisha would agree to getting a jump start on their honeymoon.

He swung open the door, ready to sweep her literally off her feet. "Oh. Lucas."

"Expecting someone else?" Lucas asked.

Christopher didn't try to hide the disappointment in his voice. "Yeah. Aisha."

Lucas pushed past Christopher and began pacing the room. "Sorry, man. But I'm in serious need of some male bonding."

Christopher shut the door. "Okay, Cabral. But if Eesh shows up, you're history."

"Got it." Lucas sprawled himself on Christopher's neatly made bed. The tragic expression on his face made him look as if he were trying to re-create the Crucifixion.

Christopher sat down on his desk chair. "What's the problem?"

Lucas moaned softly. "Has Aisha told you anything about Aaron Mendel and Zoey?"

"The poker king?" Aaron had cleaned out Christopher at cards a couple of weeks earlier, and Christopher was still bitter.

"Yeah. Has she said anything?"

"Nope."

"Come on, be straight with me," Lucas yelled, sitting up on the bed.

Christopher held up his hands. "I swear. Nothing. Believe it or not, we've had more important things on our minds than gossiping about the inhabitants of this dinky island."

Lucas banged his head twice against the wall behind Christopher's bed, leading Christopher to believe that the problem was more serious than he'd anticipated. "I caught her with him," Lucas said in a low, pained voice.

"Zoey and Aaron? What were they doing?" Christopher leaned forward in his chair, astonished.

"They were lying on her bed. Making out." Lucas made the event sound more like the bombing of Pearl Harbor than two people kissing.

"Are you sure?" Christopher asked. He didn't know what else to say.

Lucas glared at him. "If you walked into Aisha's room and found her soul-to-soul with another guy, don't you think you'd be pretty certain of what you saw?"

Christopher felt a sharp pain in his head. It had been the idea of that very vision that had made him decide to ask Aisha to marry him. "Yeah. I guess the term *innocent explanation* doesn't really apply in a case like this."

"No, *innocent* isn't the word that springs to mind. More like *sickening*." Lucas picked up Christopher's pillow, which was already flat, and began punching out what little bounce it had.

"It's not like you haven't done the same thing, Lucas. Or do I have to refresh your memory about the time you and Claire almost did the wild thang in the back of her daddy's Mercedes?"

"That was totally different," Lucas said, although

he didn't sound entirely convinced of the truth of his words.

"How so?"

"I thought Zoey was getting back together with Jake. I was angry. . . ."

"Fooling around is fooling around, Lucas. Maybe you should put your tail between your legs and beg Zoey to take you back."

Lucas's eyes flashed. "You're not exactly the first person who should be throwing stones, Shupe. How many times have you cheated on Aisha?"

"Hey, I plead no contest. But I've changed my ways. I'm a one-woman man."

Lucas rested his head in his palms. "I'm just glad Claire tipped me off. If she hadn't, I'd be walking around like a dope, the last to know that my girlfriend was with some other guy."

"How did Claire know what was going on?"

Lucas shrugged. "How does Claire know anything? She just *does*."

"Well if it makes you feel better, I don't think anyone else has a clue. Eesh would have told me."

"Not necessarily. Girls can keep secrets when they want to."

Christopher shook his head. "No way. I mean, I'm practically her fiancé—"

"What?" Lucas shrieked. For the first time since he'd walked into the room, he seemed animated.

Christopher cursed silently. He hadn't meant to tell anyone that he'd actually proposed to Aisha. On the off chance that she said no, he didn't want to look like a complete idiot. But he'd already accidentally let on to Lucas that he planned to join the army and marry Aisha. He might as well come clean now. Then he'd concentrate on damage control.

"I asked her last night."

"You're kidding."

"I've never been more serious in my life."

"What did she say?"

Again Christopher cursed himself. "Nothing yet."

Lucas put down the pillow. "Man, this is heavy."

"You're telling me," Christopher responded. His eyes darted to the phone. When would Aisha put him out of his misery?

"I hope you guys know what you're doing," Lucas said. He sounded defeated, as if the world had become too unmanageable for him to cope with anymore.

"Just do me a favor and keep your mouth shut about the whole thing. I'd like to keep my private life with Aisha *private*."

Lucas nodded. "I won't tell you if you won't."

"Deal." Christopher eyed the phone one more time.

The weekend hadn't turned out the way he'd hoped. Instead of making wedding plans with Aisha, he was moping around with Lucas Cabral. Not what he'd call an early honeymoon.

Five

Aisha lay awake in bed, staring at her digital clock. It was 5:33 A.M. At 4:04 she'd woken from a dream in which she was walking down the aisle of a church. Christopher had been waiting for her at the altar, wearing camouflage gear. He'd had an AK-47 in his hand, and Uncle Sam had been preparing to conduct the wedding ceremony. When Aisha woke, she'd been clutching the edge of her sheets as if she were holding a bouquet of flowers.

Christopher was probably near the end of his paper route by now. He got up before dawn every morning in order to earn money by delivering papers to the island residents. Gray House was his last stop, and he sometimes knocked on Aisha's window for a good-morning kiss.

Usually she welcomed the sight of Christopher at *any* time of day. But she wasn't up to seeing him right at that moment. Aisha was no closer to an answer to the Question than she'd been Saturday night. Aisha squeezed her eyes shut, willing herself to fall back to sleep.

One sheep jumped over the fence. Two sheep jumped over the fence. Three sheep jumped over the fence. . . .

She jumped when she heard a light rapping on her window. Christopher. Aisha considered pretending that she was unconscious but decided against it. Christopher would know she was faking.

She slipped quietly out of bed, then pulled on the terry-cloth robe she'd left on the chair next to her bed. The early morning air was so cold that Aisha was surprised she couldn't see her breath.

Outside the window, Christopher stood shivering in the darkness. Despite her anxiety, Aisha laughed. In a black ski mask and a navy blue parka, Christopher looked more like a burglar than a paper boy. She opened the window wide, then grabbed his hands to help him climb inside. His fingers felt like icicles.

Christopher pulled off his ski mask, revealing his beautiful face. "Thanks, Eesh," he whispered, his teeth chattering.

As she turned to shut the window, she saw Christopher's bicycle leaning against the side of the house.

"Christopher, you're freezing," Aisha said, leading him to her desk chair. She grabbed her down comforter and wrapped it around his shoulders.

"I'll warm up quick if you sit on my lap." He pulled her onto his lap, hugging her close.

Aisha yelped when Christopher's cold nose touched the sensitive skin at the nape of her neck. "Where's your car?"

"Oh, I, uh, sold it," Christopher said, sounding slightly embarrassed.

"Why?"

Island cars were something of a phenomenon. They tended to be junk heaps, little more than engines and some ripped-up upholstery. Chatham residents kept their "real" cars in parking garages in Weymouth.

"There was something I needed more than the car," Christopher said gruffly.

Aisha thought of the silver ring resting safely in its velvet box. Of course. Guilt washed over her. The whole reason that Christopher was determined to join the army was that he was poor and wanted money for an education. If she'd thought for even two seconds, she would have realized that he didn't have enough money to buy an expensive piece of jewelry.

"Oh, Christopher, you shouldn't have. . . ."

He wrapped his arms more tightly around her waist. "I wanted to, Eesh."

She pulled away from his embrace so that she could look at his face. "But—"

"I said, I *wanted* to." His voice held a warning.

Aisha bit her lip. Above all else, Christopher was proud. "Well, I love the ring. It's gorgeous."

"You're gorgeous." Christopher moved his left hand from Aisha's waist and brushed his fingers across her cheek. Gently he drew her face close to his.

Aisha shivered when she felt Christopher's soft lips. Kissing him always made her feel that the rest of the world had dropped away, leaving just the two of them standing on a cloud.

But as soon as the kiss ended, reality reared its ugly head. The temperature was below freezing, and Christopher didn't have a car. Aisha just couldn't get past the idea of his freezing his cute little butt off during a long, cold Maine winter. She had to take action.

"Hey, you know what's a funny coincidence?" she asked.

"What?" He looked skeptical, but Aisha continued.

"I was actually going to ask my parents for an island car for Christmas."

He raised an eyebrow. "Eesh, you guys already have one. Why would you want another?"

"Well, uh, you know how I'm always late for the ferry. I practically have a heart attack every morning, sprinting to the dock. If I had a car, I could, uh, drive."

Christopher laughed. "Nice try. But I'm not letting you get a car just so you can loan it to me for my paper route. No way. Uh-uh."

Aisha tried to look surprised. "Gosh, I hadn't even thought about that. But now that you mention—"

"Eesh, I didn't come here to talk about my no-car status."

She sighed, sliding down in Christopher's lap so that she could press her face against his chest rather than look him in the eye. This was the moment she'd dreaded all night.

"I know," she said softly.

"So?" The tone of his voice was light, but Aisha felt the muscles of his body tense.

"So it's a big decision, Christopher. Marriage is a big step. A huge, gigantic, mind-boggling step."

His shoulders slumped. "You don't want to marry me."

"No. I mean yes. I mean someday, definitely. But I don't know about right now."

Christopher picked up Aisha so that he could stand. Then he dropped her lightly into the chair and began pacing from her dresser to the window.

43

"Christopher, you've had time to absorb all this," Aisha went on. "I haven't."

He picked up a snow globe on Aisha's dresser. Flakes of artificial snow swirled around the miniature Empire State Building within. "I understand," he said, shaking the globe vigorously.

"You're mad." Aisha leaned her head against the back of the chair and closed her eyes for a moment. She was suddenly very tired.

"No . . ." He stopped pacing and knelt in front of Aisha. "I don't want to lose you."

A tear slid down Aisha's cheek as she ran her fingers over Christopher's short, soft hair. "You won't."

"How can you say that? You can't even decide whether or not to say yes."

"True. But there's one thing I do know."

"What?"

"I love you, Christopher."

Monday morning Jake stood alone at the rail of the *Island Breeze*, aka the *Minnow* (after the lost boat on *Gilligan's Island*). For as long as Jake could remember, he'd boarded the ferry five days a week, nine months a year, at precisely 7:39 A.M. The ride was the island's equivalent of going to school in a yellow bus.

The wind whipping over the Atlantic Ocean was freezing, but Jake welcomed the fresh air. He was still recovering from the damage he'd done to his body on Saturday night. On Sunday he'd been so tired that he'd practically had to drag his fingers across the keyboard of his computer. Even then, his English paper had fallen considerably short of the required length.

Jake turned his back to the ocean and scanned the deck. Everyone except Zoey had avoided standing on deck. She was sitting on a bench with a textbook open in her lap. Even now Jake thought she was the most attractive girl he'd ever known.

He shoved his hands deep into his pockets and walked over to her. "Hey, Zoey."

She looked up. "Oh. Hi, Jake."

"How are you?" Jake studied Zoey's face, which was pale. He also noticed that her eyes were red and puffy.

"Great. Wonderful. Deck the halls with boughs of holly. Fa la la la la, blah, blah, blah." She slammed the book shut and gave him a wry smile.

"That good, huh?" Jake sat down next to her, grateful that the wall behind the bench provided some protection from the stinging wind.

She shrugged. "Sorry. I shouldn't take my bad mood out on you."

"That's okay." Jake pulled a beat-up folder from his backpack. Inside was the extremely bad paper he'd finally written about *The Scarlet Letter*. He had a dim ray of hope that Zoey would read the approximately seven hundred words of garbage, take mercy on his sorry self, and offer to help rewrite the entire mess. It was a long shot, but he needed to pull at least a C in English in order to stay on the football team.

When Zoey didn't say anything else, he cleared his throat. "I just wanted to, uh, ask you a question. About that *Scarlet Letter* paper."

"What is it?"

"Well, like, my paper turned out to be only two and a half pages." He gestured to the folder. "Do you think that's okay?"

"You mean you haven't turned it in yet?" Zoey's voice held the incredulity that conscientious students reserved for those who were always messing up their transcripts.

"No. I've been kind of busy. . . ." His voice trailed off for a moment. He'd forgotten that Zoey had a knack for making him feel like a dog turd. "You know, helping my dad with the Christmas tree, getting ready for finals—"

"Having Lara spend the night on Saturday," Zoey added.

"How'd you know that?" Jake asked. He winced as he heard his voice crack.

Zoey waved her hand dismissively. "Long story."

He stared down at the folder. "Oh, yeah. Well."

"Jake, you know I care about you."

"Sure. I mean, you know, I care about you, too. Like, a lot." Instead of looking into her eyes, he stared at the small design on the front of her wool ski cap.

"So don't take it the wrong way when I tell you to be careful with Lara. The girl is bad news."

Jake was beginning to regret starting this conversation with Zoey. His association with Lara was the last thing he felt like talking about. Especially with Zoey, who not only was his ex-girlfriend but also had caught him confiscating all of the liquor bottles from Lara's room.

A change of subject was in order. "Are you and Lucas in a fight or something?" he asked.

Until that moment he'd been so focused on the possibility of Zoey bailing him out of academic ruin that he hadn't wondered why she wasn't making goo-goo eyes with Lucas, the way she did most mornings.

"Or something," Zoey said flatly. She opened her backpack and pulled out her French workbook.

"Want me to beat him up for you?" Jake asked.

She shook her head, looking troubled. "Will you tell me something, Jake? And be honest."

"Uh, yeah, I guess."

"Do you think I'm a bad person?"

Jake stared at her cute mittened hands and cornflower blue eyes. He could never think Zoey was a bad person, even though she had dumped him for another guy. "No."

"But I haven't been a great friend to you. I mean, I started going out with Lucas behind your back. I let on to you that your dad was having an affair. . . ."

"Zo, I'd rather not dredge up all this stuff from the past, if you don't mind."

"Sorry." She leafed absently through the pages of her workbook.

Jake took her hand (her mitten, at least) in his. "Zoey, you're an awesome person. You're a great friend, and everybody loves you."

"But I keep messing up."

"Everybody does," Jake said. He felt a knot form in his stomach as he remembered his own recent foul-up. He had a talent for messing up his own life.

She sighed deeply. "Thanks, Jake. I was hoping you'd say that."

"Hey, anytime." He withdrew his hand and stood up.

"One more thing."

"Shoot."

"I suggest that you lengthen your paper by several pages."

Jake groaned. So far, this day had lived up to the terrible reputation of Mondays everywhere.

Benjamin sat on one of the hard benches in the small, stuffy cabin of the *Island Breeze*. The ferry was always a drag, but it was worse in the winter, when freezing temperatures drove everyone inside. In past years, Benjamin had noticed that the frequency of early morning arguments increased every winter. Warm weather allowed people to work out their bad moods alone, spread out across the ferry's various decks.

As soon as he'd sat down, Benjamin had put on the earphones of his Discman. Although he wasn't listening to music, he liked the privacy that the illusion allowed. He simply didn't feel like talking. Not even to Nina.

He heard the sound of Claire's approaching footsteps but kept his face carefully neutral. As he'd hoped, she kept walking. Moments later he heard her sit down nearby. A minute passed, during which time he listened to Nina singing along to *her* Discman. From what he could tell, the song was about death, violence, and getting harassed by cops.

"Claire." Benjamin heard Lucas's voice just to his right.

"Lucas," she responded.

Benjamin tuned out Nina's voice in order to listen to Claire's conversation. His big-brother instinct told him they were going to talk about Zoey.

"I found them together," Lucas said.

Benjamin could imagine Claire's bored shrug at the revelation. "Sorry to hear that."

"Has this been going on for a while?" Lucas asked. His voice was barely above a whisper.

"I don't know, Lucas. I'm not the Liz Smith of Chatham Island."

Claire was hiding something, Benjamin was sure. The more dismissive her comments, the more she had at stake. He'd learned that fact about Claire shortly after they'd started dating.

"Come on, Claire. You knew Aaron was over at Zoey's on Saturday. Obviously you've got information."

"Look, Lucas, I don't enjoy ratting on my friends. And Zoey *is* my friend. I told you he was there because I thought you had a right to know. And because I'm positive that Zoey's in love with you. Now I'd suggest that you figure out how to remind Zoey that she's in love with you. It'll be a lot more productive than giving me the third degree."

Lucas sighed. "Well, thanks for looking out for me, Claire." He paused. "I think."

"You're welcome."

As he listened to Lucas cross to the other side of the cabin, Benjamin frowned. What was Claire up to? And how did Zoey fit in?

He was startled when Claire suddenly spoke up.

"By the way, Benjamin, I know you were listening. I haven't fallen for the earphone trick in years."

Benjamin smiled. "Good morning to you, too, Claire."

Six

Lucas jogged through the crowded Weymouth High corridor, intent on catching up with Benjamin. He hated going to Zoey's brother for information about his girlfriend's mental state, but desperate times called for desperate measures. And Lucas had been *beyond* desperate for at least the past twenty-four hours.

"Yo, man," Lucas said when he reached Benjamin's side.

"Lucas." Benjamin's tone was typically guarded. He always greeted Lucas with the caution of someone who didn't want to get caught in the middle of anything.

"I thought I'd hang with you during lunch." Lucas tried to keep his voice casual, as if he hadn't plotted for the last two hours to pump Benjamin for information.

"Cool. I always need a guide dog to get me through the cafeteria."

Lucas tried to laugh, but he sounded more like a drowning person gasping for breath. He was glad Benjamin couldn't see that he was scanning the corridor for signs of Zoey. Blind friends definitely had their advantages.

Like all of the island kids, Lucas was familiar with the routine of going through the lunch line with Benjamin. Lucas took the space in front of Benjamin, sliding his tray along the metal counter in front of plate after plate of unappetizing food. "We've got watery lasagna to your left," Lucas said. "To your right there's something that looks like it might be meat loaf. Dessert choices are blondies and fruit cup."

Benjamin and Lucas each opted for lasagna and a blondie. Lucas selected a pint of milk for himself, then searched through the drink bin for an orange juice for Benjamin.

Lucas guided Benjamin to an isolated table in the southwest corner of the cafeteria. He'd spotted Zoey, Nina, Claire, and Aisha, and he wanted to position himself in a prime spying spot.

"So, how've you been?" Lucas asked after they sat down.

Benjamin raised an eyebrow. "Fine."

Lucas waited for Benjamin to return the question, but he didn't. "Uh, are you getting nervous about the big operation?" he finally asked.

Benjamin grimaced as he swallowed his first bite of lasagna. "No. I just think about it every waking moment. No big deal."

Lucas saw an opening. It was a small, lame opening, but he'd already decided he was desperate. "I know how that is, man. I can't get this whole thing with Zoey out of my mind. It really sucks."

"Yeah, well . . ." Benjamin abandoned his lasagna and went straight for the blondie.

"So, has she, like, said anything to you? About that guy?"

"I assume you're talking about Aaron."

Lucas felt bile rise in his throat when he heard Mendel's name. He pushed his tray to the other side of the table. "Is Zoey in love with him?" he asked softly.

Benjamin snorted. "She's only known the guy for two weeks."

"Benjamin, I saw them together. They were, like, seriously making out."

"Please, Lucas, spare me the gory details. I've told you a thousand times that my sister's private life is just that. *Private*."

Lucas moaned. Benjamin was useless. "Has she said anything? One little word about how horrible she feels that we're not even on speaking terms?"

Benjamin shrugged. "Since you're such a wallowing, sorry creature, I'll take pity on you. I can faithfully report that she's miserable. She locked herself in her room all day, and I heard the distinct sound of crying. When I tried to talk to her, she told me to go away."

The news lifted Lucas's spirits a little. At least he wasn't suffering alone. Maybe there was still hope. "Thanks, Benjamin. I really needed to hear that."

"Just do me a favor and work it out. I have enough problems without having to worry about Zoey completely losing it." Benjamin sucked down the rest of his orange juice with a straw, creating a slurping sound in the bottom of the container.

Lucas picked up his blondie, slightly hungry after all. "I just hope *I* don't lose it," Lucas said.

Then he bit into a very hard piece of unidentifiable *something*, and the effort he'd made toward achieving a mood resembling something less than suicidal vanished. In Lucas's experience, cafeterias tended to have that effect on people.

*　*　*

Claire surveyed the faces of Nina, Zoey, and Aisha. They were all eating mechanically, and Nina hadn't offered up even one nauseating description of lasagna. She knew why Zoey was upset, but what about Aisha and Nina? They usually couldn't shut up. Someone, namely Claire, needed to probe the situation.

"So, Nina, how are you enjoying that lasagna?" Claire asked.

Nina's fork froze in midair. She looked at the processed cheese that was dangling from her utensil and made a gagging motion. "Gee, Claire, I hadn't noticed how much it resembled decomposed entrails until you forced me to stop and evaluate. Thanks."

"My pleasure, sister dear," Claire said. She waited for Nina to say something else, but Nina just put down her fork and slid the tray of food to the other side of the table. Strange. Nina usually said funny things in threes, least funny to most funny, following what she called the rule of comic tautology. But just then she'd stopped at one.

Claire tried again. "Aisha, have you started studying for history yet?"

"Studying?" Aisha asked blankly.

"We've got exams starting Wednesday, in case you'd forgotten."

Aisha nodded. "Oh, right. Exams. This week's going to suck."

Claire wondered if some evil school administrator had started handing out Xanax while she wasn't looking. She'd never seen a group of people so totally zoned out. "What about you, Zoey?"

Zoey shrugged. "Exams are the least of my worries. My plan is to cram, spill out everything I know during the tests, then promptly forget what I've learned."

"The American system of education at its finest," Nina commented.

Claire actually felt relieved to hear one of her sister's sarcastic remarks. A silent Nina was a disturbing Nina.

"Well, I think *The Scarlet Letter* and *Othello* are going to be a big part of the English final," Claire said to Zoey. "I heard there's a whole essay on the topic of adultery."

Claire watched, mildly amused, as Zoey's face turned first pale, then red. She was sure that visions of Lucas's stricken face were dancing in Zoey's head.

"Hey, what're Lucas and Benjamin talking about over there?" Aisha asked, as if on cue. "Lucas looks pretty intense."

Claire knew when her work was done. She picked up her tray. "Maybe the rest of you don't care about getting into a good college, but I'm going to the library."

As she walked away from the table, Claire glanced quickly toward the corner where Benjamin and Lucas were sitting. Lucas looked like Bill Bixby just before he would turn green and pop out of his clothes on *The Incredible Hulk*.

Yes, Lucas's anger over seeing Aaron and Zoey together was going to keep Zoey plenty busy. Claire hadn't gotten anywhere with Aaron at Sunday brunch—parents had been in the vicinity all through the eggs Benedict. But she would have more than enough time to go in for the proverbial kill after exams were over.

Seven

As the *Minnow* pulled into Chatham Island Monday afternoon, Zoey took a deep breath, then exhaled slowly. She couldn't allow the cold war between her and Lucas to continue. His icy stares in French class had been so disturbing that she'd forgotten how to conjugate the verb *être* for the first time since first-year French. She wanted a peace agreement, and she wanted it that day.

The second the ferry stopped moving, Lucas darted down the gangplank. Without saying goodbye to anyone, he headed quickly up Dock Street toward home. Zoey chased after him, her backpack bumping against her thigh as she ran. At the corner of South Street, Lucas stopped to tie his shoe. Zoey moved in.

"Lucas, we've got to talk about this," she announced.

Lucas finished tying his lace and stood up. "What is there to say?"

"I don't know. . . ." Zoey shifted her backpack from one hand to the other, then back again. What was there to say, anyway? A simple apology wasn't going to wipe out what had happened.

Lucas's dark eyes glittered resentfully as he stared

at her. "Are you going to tell me that it didn't mean anything? That you were wishing he was me the whole time you two were exchanging saliva?"

"I don't *know*." Zoey felt paralyzed. She realized now that she should have prepared a speech.

Lucas pressed his lips into a thin, tight line. "Or maybe this was a final act of revenge. To get back at me for fooling around with Claire."

Zoey thought of Aaron's beautiful face and husky voice. An act of revenge? She wished she could tell Lucas that Aaron had meant nothing to her—that he was simply a tool to give Lucas a taste of his own humiliating medicine. But she'd lied enough. She couldn't look Lucas in the eye and tell him something that in her heart she knew was untrue.

"No, it wasn't like that," she said quietly.

Lucas snorted. "Great. So it *did* mean something. That's beautiful, Zoey."

Tears welled in Zoey's eyes. How could she explain? "Lucas, if you keep attacking me, this conversation is going to go nowhere."

"I suppose if I were Aaron, we could dispense with conversation altogether. We could just play tongue hockey."

"Being vulgar isn't going to make things better."

Lucas grabbed Zoey's arm in a tight grip. "What is going to make things better?"

"Lucas, I don't know." Zoey had lost track of how many times she'd repeated that phrase, but her brain simply wasn't supplying any answers.

"This isn't just about you and that pretentious jerk, Zo. It's about a lot of things."

Zoey nodded. Lucas was right. If their relationship had been perfect to begin with, she never would have been attracted to Aaron. At least she wouldn't have *acted* on her attraction. But she was in love with Lucas. The misery she'd endured for the past two days had convinced her of that fact. "Maybe if we sit down and really do some communicating—"

"Jeez, Zo. You sound like a crackpot pop psychologist."

Zoey felt the anger that had been slowly rising to the surface begin to boil. "I forgot I was talking to Mr. Perfect," she yelled. "For some stupid reason I was under the illusion that I was speaking with my cheating, immature sex maniac of a boyfriend."

Lucas grabbed Zoey's other arm, shaking her hard. "Don't you dare turn this around on me, Zoey."

"Lucas, you're scaring me." She'd never seen Lucas enraged. His face was turning purple, and his pupils were dilated. Zoey felt a flash of fear.

In the next moment he released his hold on her. She stumbled backward, set off balance by the sudden absence of his grip.

"Yeah?" he said, crossing his arms in front of his chest. "Well, you're scaring me, too, Zoey."

"We can work it out, Lucas."

"Are you sure, Zoey? Are you sure that's what you really want?"

"I was. Before this conversation started."

"Listen, I can't deal with this right now. I've got to think about exams."

"Lucas . . ."

He turned to leave. "Don't call me, I'll call you."

Zoey watched numbly as Lucas sprinted up South Street. When he got to the corner, Zoey allowed the tears to flow.

*   *   *

At eight o'clock that evening Benjamin stood outside Zoey's door, debating whether or not he should knock. On the one hand, he didn't like to interfere in her life. On the other hand, she hadn't come out since she'd run into the house after school and raced straight to her room. He was worried.

He knocked lightly. "Zo, it's me," he called.

"Just a minute." From inside, he heard the muffled sound of crying, followed by a hiccup and a nose being blown.

"Can I come in now?"

"Yeah."

Benjamin walked into Zoey's room and made his way to the edge of her bed. "I had an interesting talk with Lucas today."

She blew her nose again. "How much did he tell you?"

"Enough."

"Does Nina know?"

"Uh-uh," he said, shaking his head. "I figured you'd tell her when you're ready."

"Thanks for keeping your mouth shut. I'm not in the mood to be headlining the scandal of the week."

"Now you know how Oprah feels."

"So, are you going to give me a lecture?" she asked sullenly.

Benjamin reached toward the sound of her voice and patted her awkwardly on the shoulder. "Since when do I give my little sister lectures?"

"Since she started acting like Public Enemy Number One."

Behind his dark glasses, Benjamin rolled his eyes. "Zoey, kissing a guy who isn't your boyfriend hardly qualifies you for the FBI's ten-most-wanted list."

She sighed deeply. "I've just never been so confused in my life."

"What about when you were seeing Lucas behind Jake's back? That must have been confusing."

"No. Because I knew that I was really in love with Lucas. Jake and I were going to break up . . . it was just a matter of time."

"So? How do you feel now?"

"I'm still in love with Lucas."

"What about Aaron?"

He imagined Zoey shaking her head helplessly. After several seconds she spoke. "I've been trying to resist my attraction to him. Really. I even wrote him a note saying we couldn't talk anymore. But . . ."

"But it just sort of happened."

"Right. And now I don't know what to do."

Benjamin weighed his words carefully. If he judged Zoey for what she'd done, she'd feel even worse. And he'd learned that when people were criticized for their actions, they had a habit of responding by doing the same action, only worse.

"You could have talked to me about it, Zoey. Before you got in over your head."

"You have enough on your mind, Benjamin."

He tried to laugh. "Who, me? I'm footloose and fancy-free."

"You can quit with the Superman act, Benjamin. I know you're worried about the surgery."

"I thought we were supposed to be talking about your messed-up life, not mine."

"Fine, Benjamin. If you want to keep all of your anxieties bottled up, be my guest."

"Hey, don't get testy. I just want to know what you're going to do about this *thing* with Aaron."

"Well, Aaron's going to be gone in a few weeks."

"Aha! The old out-of-sight-out-of-mind philosophy."

"It's not like that, Benjamin."

Benjamin knew when to give in. Zoey wasn't looking for solutions. In fact, she almost seemed to be enjoying her state of misery. He'd been depressed enough times to know that occasionally people had to suffer alone until they were ready to find their way toward happiness. Apparently Zoey was in that masochistic category. He stood up to leave.

"I've made my prognosis."

"What is it?"

"You'll survive, Zo."

She groaned. "I guess I don't have any choice."

Benjamin walked toward the door, then stopped. "By the way, did Nina, uh, say anything to you?"

"About what?"

"Oh, nothing. Nothing at all. Never mind."

Benjamin closed the door softly behind him, then stood for a few moments in the hall. Zoey hadn't told Nina about Aaron. Nina hadn't told Zoey about having sex. Why?

He'd always been under the impression that girls shared every little detail of their lives. After all, he'd been subjected to more than a few conversations about the relative merits of Tampax versus Kotex. But apparently he'd been wrong. As it turned out, girls were just as complicated and secretive as their male counterparts.

Benjamin nodded thoughtfully. Interesting.

Eight

Tuesday afternoon Nina smiled as Benjamin put his arm around her shoulder and pulled her close. The ferry was nearing Chatham Island, and all she could think about was being alone with Benjamin.

"Do you have to go study now?" Benjamin asked.

Nina thought of her English exam, which would take place in less than twenty-four hours. She still had to read *Brave New World*. "I can't study until after *Jeopardy!* It's a biorhythm thing."

"You know, we haven't been, um, together since the hotel."

Nina felt herself blush. "Oh, really? I hadn't noticed."

"Well, I have." Benjamin moved his hand to the back of Nina's neck. "So what do you say?"

"Your place or mine, sailor?"

The ferry docked, and Nina and Benjamin started walking slowly toward the gangplank.

"Yours." He pulled her to a stop and gave her a soft kiss on the lips. "But I'll meet you there. I've got to stop by the restaurant first."

Nina watched Benjamin walk away, noting what a great butt he had. She jumped when Zoey and Ai-

61

sha appeared on either side of her. She sent up a silent prayer that neither one had developed ESP. She wasn't ready to share her X-rated thoughts about Benjamin.

"There's no way I can study right now," Zoey said.

Aisha nodded. "Me neither. I think I need a bag of nacho-cheese-flavored Doritos and some ice cream before I can even think about our exam tomorrow."

"Let's hit my kitchen. My mom and dad are both at the restaurant."

"Sounds like a plan," Aisha agreed.

"Want to come, Nina?" Zoey asked.

"I'll take a pass on the binge-and-purge session, thanks."

Aisha raised her eyebrows. "Don't tell me you're rushing home to study."

Nina felt the blush creeping back up to the surface. "No, uh, actually, Benjamin's coming over."

"Well, excuse us," Zoey said. "We didn't realize that you don't have time for your best friends anymore."

"Hey, I'm just making up for all those years when you would disappear to *Joke's* house for, like, days on end."

Zoey shrugged. "Just don't do anything I wouldn't do."

Nina stood still as Aisha and Zoey headed in the direction of the Passmores'. If Zoey knew how apt that particular remark was, her head would probably explode. Especially considering the fact that Nina was not just doing the things Zoey wouldn't do, but was doing them with Zoey's own *brother*. Nina shook her head, wondering at what exact moment her boyfriend had taken her best friend's place as number one confidante. On second thought, she realized that she *did* know the precise moment: late one night in the Malibu Hotel.

Zoey and Aisha sat at the Passmores' kitchen table, which was currently littered with several bags of potato chips, a box of Pop-Tarts, and a pint of Ben & Jerry's Chunky Monkey.

Aisha picked up a pretzel and stuck her left ring finger through one of the loops. *Anything*, she realized, could be used as an engagement ring . . . if a person was engaged. She stared at her hand as if the pretzel would offer an answer to her dilemma.

Across the table, Zoey sighed dramatically. Aisha then watched with surprise as Zoey pitched forward and banged her head against the table.

"What's wrong with you? Did you eat too many Pop-Tarts or something?"

"I have a confession," Zoey muttered to the surface of the table.

"Aha! I knew you were the one who stole the hairbrush out of my gym locker."

When Zoey sat up, her hair was in her face. She didn't bother to brush it aside. "Ha, ha, ha."

"Gee, Zo. Your holiday cheer is making me giddy."

"This is serious, Eesh." Zoey pulled the ice cream toward her, as if for reinforcement.

Aisha took the pretzel off her finger and snapped it in two. "Okay, my child. Confess. Then I'll tell you how many Hail Marys to do for your penance."

"I really hope you're not planning a career as a stand-up comedian." Zoey started to spoon up a bite of Chunky Monkey.

"Hey, I'm just trying to make up for Nina's absence," Aisha said indignantly.

"I appreciate the effort, but even Nina isn't Nina these days."

Aisha considered the observation. Aisha had been so wrapped up in her own life that she hadn't been paying attention to anyone else's. But once Zoey mentioned it, Aisha realized that Nina had indeed been extremely quiet for the past few days. Decidedly un-Nina-like behavior.

"True," Aisha agreed finally. "Now, let's cut the chitchat. What did you do that's making you look so guilty?"

"I fooled around with Aaron."

The pretzel crumbled in Aisha's hand. "What? I don't think I heard you right."

"You heard me. And I did it more than once."

"Wow! And I was sorry that I missed *Melrose Place* last night."

"There's more," Zoey groaned. She tried to bang her head against the table again, but her forehead hit the ice cream.

Aisha passed Zoey a roll of paper towels from the counter. "What is it?"

"Lucas caught us. He walked into my room while Aaron and I were kissing." She wiped her forehead, then frowned at the ice-cream residue on the paper towel. "I'm pathetic."

Aisha exhaled slowly. "Were you standing up, at least?"

Zoey shook her head. "We were lying on my bed."

"Wow," Aisha repeated.

"Yeah."

Aisha picked up a potato chip and crunched

thoughtfully. "You know, maybe human beings weren't really created to be faithful to one person for their entire lives. I mean, when marriage was invented, how long did people live? Till they were thirty? Maybe forty, tops?"

"What's your point?"

"Knowing that we're probably going to live to be eighty or ninety, maybe we shouldn't get married until we're around sixty."

"Are you serious?"

"No. Yes. I don't know."

Zoey gave her a searching look. "I thought you were way into the one-guy-one-girl equation. Why the sudden meditation on monogamy?"

"Christopher proposed."

"Aisha Gray, you've been sitting here letting me babble on about my mundane boyfriend problems, and the whole time you had, like, the biggest news *ever*!"

"What should I have said? 'Christopher is joining the army and wants me to marry him and go along for the ride. Please pass the Pop-Tarts'?"

"The *army?*" Zoey's jaw dropped.

Aisha felt a huge lump form in her throat. Saying out loud that Christopher had decided to join the army somehow made it true. Up until that moment she'd forced that detail of his proposal to the back of her mind. "He wants money for college," Aisha said flatly.

Zoey reached over and squeezed Aisha's hand. "What are you going to say?"

The two pounds of junk food Aisha had consumed in the last fifteen minutes churned in her stomach. She shook her head. "That's the problem. I don't know."

Zoey propped her chin in her hands and stared at the carton of Chunky Monkey as if it were a crystal ball. "I thought high school was supposed to be about proms and cheerleading. Why is everything so incredibly complicated?"

As the opening music for *Jeopardy!* began, Benjamin nudged Nina. "I'm sorry about . . . you know. What *didn't* take place in your room."

Nina shrugged. "Hey, it happens all the time. At least that's what I hear."

"I'm just so nervous about the surgery. . . ."

Nina gave him a loud kiss on the cheek. "The fact that I kept getting up to make sure I'd locked my door probably didn't help any."

"Still, I feel like a loser," Benjamin admitted.

"Benjamin, you've apologized fifteen times. Just let it go."

Benjamin sighed. "I'm gonna take off."

"Okay."

"But, uh, first I've got to talk to Claire."

"I hope you're not planning to discuss our sex life," Nina said.

Or lack thereof, Benjamin mentally added. "No, it's, uh, about a class."

"Well, while you're up there, feel around for voodoo dolls." He sensed her turning back to the television set. "I'll take U.S. history for a hundred, Alex," she said.

Benjamin laughed as he walked toward the staircase. Only Nina could make him smile after one of the most humiliating nonevents of his life.

Benjamin felt a sense of déjà vu as he climbed the stairs that led to Claire's third-floor bedroom. He hadn't been up there since they'd broken up, during the first week of school.

"Hello, Claire."

"Benjamin. It's been a long time since you darkened my doorstep."

"Am I still welcome?"

"Are you kidding? As my deranged sister's boyfriend, you're practically family."

Benjamin walked into the room. He still remembered how many steps there were between the door and Claire's desk (five) and between the door and the chair (six), as well as how many steps it took to get to the ladder that led to her widow's walk (twelve). Benjamin didn't let himself recall the number of paces to her bed (nine).

"Speaking of Nina, she's convinced that you've bugged her room."

"Frankly, I'm surprised she actually let you come up here without a chaperon."

"She trusts me. And you, believe it or not."

Claire laughed contemptuously. "So, has my dear sibling finally driven you over the edge? Are you here to beg to get me back?"

Benjamin put his hand over his heart. "Stop. I can't take all the warm fuzzies you're sending my way."

"We've never been big on small talk, Benjamin. Why don't you tell me what's on your mind?"

Benjamin walked slowly to Claire's chair. He never knew when someone was going to unexpectedly rearrange their furniture.

"It's in the same place," she said.

"Thanks." He sat down. "I'm worried about Zoey."

"From what I hear, Zoey's doing pretty well for

herself." He heard the bed squeak quietly as Claire sat down.

"So you've just heard what Zoey's been up to."

"It's a small island."

"She belongs with Lucas," Benjamin said simply.

Claire was quiet for a moment. "I couldn't agree more. But who she sees is her decision entirely."

As always, Claire wasn't going to make things easy. Benjamin decided to go for the throat. Claire was most vulnerable when caught by surprise.

"You want Aaron for yourself, Claire. Admit it."

"Benjamin the matchmaker. I never thought I'd see the day."

Benjamin smiled as he heard the trace of nervousness in her voice. Until that moment his idea that Claire was into Aaron had been just a hunch. Now he was positive.

"A good relationship does strange things to people," he said.

"I wouldn't know."

Benjamin let that one pass. He stood up. "Listen, Claire, I know you're up to something. And I have a feeling that it involves you getting Aaron for yourself, which would then allow Zoey and Lucas to go back to being a blissed-out couple."

"Very insightful," Claire commented.

"Just get on with the plan, Claire. I can't stand to hear my sister sobbing in her bedroom day after day."

He walked toward the door, satisfied that Claire was indirectly going to solve Zoey's problems.

"Hey, Benjamin?" Claire called.

He turned. "Yeah?"

"Good luck with the surgery."

Nine

On the way home from Zoey's, Aisha made a detour. When she'd been filling Zoey in on the proposal (and swearing her to secrecy), she'd neglected to mention a few details. Like the fact that she'd avoided Christopher since he'd shown up at her house the day before.

As Aisha climbed the stairs to Christopher's small studio in one of the island's few low-rent boarding houses, she practiced her speech. She had to be firm yet gentle. Despite the large size of Christopher's ego, he could be quite sensitive.

Aisha frowned as she knocked on the door. From inside she could hear the raspy voice of Billie Holiday. Christopher only listened to Billie when he was depressed. "Be strong, Eesh," she muttered. She took a deep breath and knocked again.

Inside, the music went off. Christopher came to the door wearing only a worn pair of sweatpants. Aisha gasped at the sight of his broad, dark chest. He looked gorgeous.

"So you finally got my four phone messages?" he asked.

Her smile wavered. "I'm sorry. I just . . ."

"Needed to think?" he asked. "Some more?"

She nodded. "Can I come in?"

He stepped back, and she walked into his sparsely furnished room. There were only two places to sit— a chair and the bed. Aisha reluctantly chose the chair.

"Are you trying to tell me something, Aisha? Like I should get lost?"

"No, of course not." How could she make him understand? "Christopher, I've thought about nothing but the possibility of us getting married ever since you asked. But I can't decide right now."

"Why not?" He still hadn't sat down, and his looming presence was making it difficult for Aisha to remember her speech.

"Because I've got exams. And then I have to get ready for Christmas. You know, we're going to have that big party at Gray House. . . ."

"In other words, everything in your life is more important than I am."

"You know it's not like that," she responded hotly.

He collapsed on the bed. "I'm sorry, Aisha. But you know I'm not a patient guy."

She stood up and moved to the bed. Guys tended to take things better if they felt desired. Aisha sat down behind Christopher and slipped her arms around his waist. She rested her cheek against the smooth skin of his back. "Christopher, when I see you, all logic flies out of my head. And right now I can't afford that. This is going to be the last set of grades I get before applying to college."

"What're you saying?"

She tightened her arms. "I love you, but I can't see you this week. Or talk to you. Until Friday."

"Aisha, this is crazy."

"Please, Christopher," she begged. "If I see you, all I'll be able to think about is *us*. And right now I need to think about English and history and calculus."

She felt his muscles relax. He took her hands and moved so that he could face her. "And then you'll give me an answer?"

"And then I'll *think* about the answer."

"Okay, Eesh. But you'd better give me one hell of a good-night kiss. Especially if it has to last until Friday."

Aisha gave herself a mental pat on the back. Firm yet gentle had worked. Really, men could be surprisingly understanding at times—as long as they were approached on their own level.

At 10:58 P.M. Jake turned off his computer. He'd stretched his *Scarlet Letter* paper out another five pages with the help of a few new ideas and the use of words such as *very* and *seemingly*.

Jake stood up and shook out his arms and legs, which ached from sitting so long. Unfortunately, he still had a semester's worth of the English notes he'd photocopied from Zoey to study before he could consider himself prepared for the English exam.

Sighing, Jake flopped onto his bed and opened his notebook. For several minutes he stared at the page, but nothing happened. His mind was exhausted from writing the paper.

Jake closed his eyes, trying to relax. A minute passed. His leg twitched, and he felt a sharp pain in the palm of his hand. Jake rolled over, groaning. There was no way he'd be able to study those notes that night.

He'd be best off if he went to sleep right away,

then got up at the crack of dawn to study. But even though his brain was fried, his body was still wide awake. He needed something to make him tired.

Ever since Saturday night, he'd resisted the urge to have another drink. And he'd been fine. He hadn't even been seriously tempted. Just a little tempted. Maybe, he thought, he'd kicked his drinking habit to the point where he could have a beer now and then.

Jake sat up, considering the possibility. An alcoholic was someone who *needed* to drink. He didn't need to. He'd proven that more than once. And there was nothing wrong with relaxing with a nice, cold beer after a hard day. His dad did it all the time. Most parents did.

Jake jumped from the bed and went to his door. He'd have one beer. One lousy twelve-ounce can of beer. Then he'd be able to go to sleep. The beer would actually *help* him with his English exam, now that he really thought about it.

Jake went into the hall and headed for the stairs. His room was in the basement of the house and accessible by a sliding glass door, a fact that he'd learned to appreciate. Visitors could come and go from his room without his parents ever knowing. On Sunday morning, for instance, Mrs. McRoyan had had no idea that Lara was in the house.

Jake walked upstairs, thinking of Lara. He'd heard nothing from her since they'd woken up in bed together. He hoped she hadn't been drinking. Unlike him, she really seemed to have a problem.

When he walked into the kitchen, Jake's heart sank. ''Hey, Dad,'' he said, trying not to sound disappointed.

Mr. McRoyan looked up from the newspaper he

was reading at the kitchen table. "Hi, Jake. How's the studying going?"

"Good. I just, uh, came up here to get some juice."

"A little vitamin C, huh?"

"Yep." Jake opened the refrigerator door. His eyes lingered on a six-pack of Beck's. He forced himself to take out the orange juice.

"Want me to quiz you for a while?" Mr. Mc-Royan asked as Jake poured the juice into a glass.

Jake thought again of the beer. "Ah, no, thanks, Dad. I'm doing fine on my own." He started toward the door.

"Well, I'll be up a little while longer in case you change your mind."

"Yeah. Thanks."

Back in his room, Jake stared at the telephone. Lara might have some beer. Probably not, but there was always the chance. She hadn't entirely convinced Jake that she wasn't going to take a sip or two now and then.

But he couldn't call. One of the Passmores would definitely answer the phone, since Lara's garage room didn't have an extension. And Zoey had just given him a lecture about Lara. He wasn't up for another.

Jake grabbed his coat. He'd simply jog over to the Passmores' and say hi to Lara. If she happened to have some stray beers around, maybe he'd have one. If not, the night air would probably do him some good.

And he'd still get home in plenty of time to grab a few hours of sleep. He'd be in great shape for studying in the morning. Jake grinned. A plan was a very good thing.

A look at exams
(otherwise known as the condoned, ritualistic torture of defenseless high-school students)

Wednesday, December 18
9:15 A.M.

Zoey, Claire, Aisha, Jake, and Lucas report to the Weymouth High cafeteria, where all seniors are being given their final English examination.

Claire breezes through the true-false section in exactly twelve minutes. She spends twenty minutes on each of the three essay questions, then leaves the cafeteria with eighteen minutes to spare.

As soon as Jake sees the test, he curses himself for having gone to see Lara. She'd had beer—a whole twelve-pack of Budweiser. He ended up getting only three hours of sleep, and now he has a hangover. Needless to say, he didn't get up early to go over Zoey's notes.

Jake guesses on thirty of the forty true-false questions. He isn't sure how long each of his essays should be but decides that short and sweet is as good a strategy as any. Knowing when to give up, he leaves the exam fifteen minutes early, just behind Claire.

* * *

74

Zoey completes the true-false section quickly. She then stares at the first essay question for five minutes: "Address the theme of adultery and betrayal in at least three of the works we've read this semester."

For the next forty minutes she writes the most insightful essay of her life (which is liberally sprinkled with badly disguised autobiographical incidents). She scrawls out the remaining two essays in fifteen minutes each, then leaves the exam wondering if there is such a thing as a redo.

Aisha is in a different class, and her exam has no true-false questions. She completes the multiple-choice portion of her exam in ten minutes, then moves on to identifications. She spends the remainder of her allotted ninety minutes writing an essay about William Butler Yeats's abiding, lifelong passion for a woman named Maude Gonne, who wouldn't marry him. She ends the essay by stating that it is her personal belief that Maude would have married William if only he hadn't tried to push her into the commitment before she was ready. She then leaves the exam with Zoey, who seems distraught.

Lucas tries hard to concentrate on his exam, which has a true-false section, multiple-choice questions, identifications, *and* an essay. But he finds himself spending several minutes at a time staring at Zoey, who is all the way on the other side of the cafeteria.

By the time he gets to his essay, he decides to ignore the question, which is about loneliness in *Robinson Crusoe*. Instead, he writes about how Othello must have felt when he thought Desdemona had fooled around behind his back.

On his way out, Lucas explains to Mr. Swenson that he'd misread the question. Mr. Swenson gives him a strange look but says he'll give Lucas a break, since *Othello* was a perfectly valid work to write about.

1:00 P.M.

Benjamin reports to Mrs. Daily's classroom. She asks Benjamin to identify fifteen characters from books he's read during the past semester. He knows ten cold, guesses on three, and has to admit on two that he has absolutely no idea. He realizes that the two he doesn't know are from books Nina read to him when they first started going out and tended to lose their concentration. However, he keeps this particular bit of information to himself.

Mrs. Daily then instructs him to give an oral essay on the nature and consequences of risk-taking in at least three works he's studied since September. Benjamin speaks eloquently and passionately for fifteen minutes, until Mrs. Daily finally tells him to shut up. She then informs Benjamin that he's gotten an A.

On his way out the door, she wishes him good luck with his impending surgery.

Thursday, December 19
9:15 A.M.

Nina stomps into the Weymouth High cafeteria, where all juniors are scheduled to take their English exams. She puts in a request to take her test in the school library, on the grounds that no one should have to spend an entire hour and a half near so much rotting food. Her request is denied.

Nina then tries very hard to concentrate on the use of metaphor in *Cry, the Beloved Country* but keeps being distracted by the smell of the lunchroom.

She moves on to the topic of desire in *Romeo and Juliet* but is preoccupied with the fact that Benjamin hasn't wanted to have sex with her again.

By the time she turns in her test, she's decided she needs to buy *The Joy of Sex* and get some pointers.

Friday, December 20
10:00 A.M.

Zoey enters the room in which she will take her French exam. Lucas has not yet arrived. She chooses a desk that is surrounded by empties, just in case Lucas wants to sit next to her. Or in front of her. Or behind her.

10:03 A.M.

Lucas walks into the French exam, totally unprepared. He sits as far away from Zoey as possible. He has two reasons for this: (1) he wants to make her feel bad, and (2) he's learned from the English exam that if she's in his line of vision, his concentration is shot.

10:15 A.M.–11:45 A.M.

Zoey and Lucas each conjugate a dozen French verbs. Zoey messes up the subjunctive. Lucas messes up the pluperfect.

Ten

Friday afternoon Zoey sat behind the cash register at Passmores'. There were no customers in the restaurant, and she still had another three hours before her shift was over. At that rate, her tip would amount to about five measly dollars by the time she was done.

She picked up a menu, then tossed it aside. She'd long since memorized every item of food Passmores' served. There was nothing there to keep her interested. She sighed heavily. The only thing she had to do was contemplate the disaster of a life she'd created for herself.

"Got those waitress blues?" Zoey recognized the low, husky voice instantly.

She jumped. "Aaron! I didn't hear you come in."

"I hope I'm not disturbing you."

Zoey came out from behind the register. She gestured toward the empty tables. "You can see how packed we are."

He laughed. "Can I buy a cup of coffee? I swear I'll give you a big tip."

"Hey, it's on the house." Zoey grabbed the coffeepot and a pitcher of cream. "Sit down."

Zoey tried to keep her back to Aaron as she

78

poured the coffee. Her hands were shaking, and she felt short of breath. Finally she put the coffee in front of him and sat down at the next table.

"I've picked up the phone to call you at least twenty times," Aaron said. He was staring straight into her eyes.

"Really?" Zoey squeaked.

"Yeah." As he stirred cream into his cup, Zoey noticed for the hundredth time what beautiful hands he had. "But I knew you had exams. I figured you needed to study."

"I did. I mean, that's why I haven't called you, either. I was studying." *And thinking about you. And Lucas. And me.*

"I'm really sorry I fouled up your life."

"You didn't," Zoey insisted.

"The other thing I kept asking myself when I wanted to call you was, 'What if Lucas is there? How's that going to look?' "

Zoey took a straw from her apron pocket and began bending it around her finger. She had no idea how she wanted this conversation to go. "Lucas hasn't set foot in my house since, uh, you know."

"I'm sorry, Zoey."

The straw unbent and fell to the floor. "Don't apologize. It's not your fault."

He frowned at his coffee. "Of course it is. I never should have come over on Saturday."

She picked up the straw, then moved to sit across from him. "Hey, *I'm* the horrible person who fooled around behind my boyfriend's back. You weren't doing anything wrong."

When he looked up at her, his hazel eyes seemed to penetrate her soul. "You could never be horrible, Zoey. You're perfect."

She shook her head. Why couldn't Lucas say things like that? If he'd been as nice about what had happened as Aaron was being, they'd already be back together. But no. Lucas had to make her feel like a felon for being attracted to another guy.

"I'm not even *close* to perfect, Aaron. Compared to you, I'm a total basket case."

He smiled, showing his perfect white teeth. "No, I'm weak, Zoey. At this moment all I want to do is ask you to come over and celebrate the first night of your vacation with me."

Zoey gasped. What was she going to say to that? "Aaron—"

"But I'm not going to," he continued. "Because you're a loyal girlfriend, and I know that you'd say no."

Zoey felt even worse. She'd been seriously considering saying yes. Aaron stood up.

"Thanks for the coffee."

"Oh, ah, you're welcome."

"I guess I'll see you at the Grays' Christmas Eve party."

Zoey nodded. "Yeah."

"I'll try not to make trouble for you and Lucas."

With that, Aaron turned and walked out of Passmores'. Zoey sat dumbly. She was glad that Aaron had made the decision between him and Lucas so simple . . . but suddenly she wasn't sure it was the *right* decision.

Of course, she still had the remaining two hours and forty-five minutes of her shift to analyze this new development.

In the fading afternoon light, Claire opened her journal. She pulled her wool hat further over her ears, then uncapped the pen she'd brought up to the widow's walk from her room.

Friday, December 21. Still no rain or snow, although clouds are low, as if gathered for an impending storm. Weather fronts seem to be against me this season — so far, no activity worth mentioning.

Today marks the beginning of Christmas vacation, which I am confident will prove more interesting than the weather. Having aced my exams, I can turn all of my attention to Aaron

"Hi, Claire."

Claire dropped her pen and slammed her journal shut. The subject of her journal entry, Aaron Mendel himself, was on the ladder that led to her widow's walk. Only his head was visible above the roof of the house.

"Do you always sneak up on people when they're in the midst of recording their private thoughts?" Claire asked testily.

He grinned. "Only when I think those thoughts might prove titillating," he responded.

Aaron continued up the ladder and hoisted himself onto the roof. In faded Levi's and a wool plaid shirt, he looked even more incredible than usual. Claire stood and moved to the railing of the widow's walk. Her heart was pounding in a ridiculous manner, and she felt extremely conscious of the ugly orange hat on her head. On Zoey, a hat like that would be cute. On Claire, it was entirely out of place.

"So, long time no see," Aaron said, coming up beside her. "We missed you at dinner the other night."

Claire shrugged. "I thought I should study."

Actually, she'd made a strategic decision to avoid Aaron. When he'd made no effort to be alone with her at brunch on Sunday, she'd realized that she'd been too available for the past few weeks. Once she wasn't around, Aaron would wonder about her absence. Which meant he'd have to think about her. Apparently her tactic had been at least partially successful.

"So, did you ace your exams?" he asked.

"Yes."

He cleared his throat. "We didn't really have a chance to talk when my mom and I came over for brunch on Sunday."

"You noticed."

"I try to notice everything, Claire." His voice was low . . . almost seductive. Claire's insides seemed to be melting at an alarming rate.

"Oh, really? I'm intrigued. Tell me more."

"My mom mentioned that you stopped by Gray House on Saturday night."

"That's right. I did." Claire tried to look bored. She wasn't thrilled that Aaron knew she'd gone looking for him. Of course, there hadn't been any doubt that his blabbermouth mother would fill him in.

"That was awfully thoughtful of you," Aaron said blandly.

"Claire Geiger aims to please."

Aaron was quiet for a moment. "She said she ran into you around ten o'clock."

Claire raised an eyebrow. She'd expected Aaron to find out about her fateful visit to Gray House. She'd even thought he *might* figure out that she'd told Lucas he was over at Zoey's. But she hadn't thought he'd confront her with it. She was impressed.

"Mmm. Sounds about right."

Aaron's hazel eyes bored into hers. "Lucas showed up at Zoey's at five after ten."

Claire smiled. "Did he? I'll have to write that one in my diary."

"Don't play games with me, Claire."

"I don't think *I'm* the one playing games."

"What does that mean?"

"Aaron, you know Zoey has a boyfriend. Yet you continue to pursue her. Your innocent act might fool others, but I'm a little smarter than that."

He took a step closer, and she could smell his coconut-scented shampoo. "Tell me, Claire," he said softly. "Why do you care whether or not I'm with Zoey?"

She stepped backward. "Most people would assume that I'm just looking out for the welfare of one of my best friends."

Aaron laughed. "Right."

"Then again, I suppose it's possible I have an ulterior motive."

"You're not going to make me guess, are you?"

Claire let her gaze rest on Aaron's full, red lips. "No, you don't have to guess. I'll tell you." She started to walk away, then turned. "But not until I'm ready."

As Claire hurried down the ladder that led to her bedroom, she heard Aaron's deep, rich laughter from above. *Soon, Aaron*, she thought. *Soon the game will be over.*

Or just beginning, depending on how one looked at it.

The first night of
Christmas vacation

Benjamin went over to Nina's. They spent four hours in Nina's room, during which time Nina expressed her many insecurities in regard to her relationship with Benjamin. After he assured her that he was still in love with her, and would be after his surgery, they had sex for the second time ever. This time Benjamin had no trouble. Afterward, Nina felt very cozy and loved. But there was a hollow place inside her that was still convinced Benjamin would dump her as soon as he got his sight back.

Claire read a book called *What You Don't Know About Your Atmosphere*. Every so often she wondered if Zoey and Lucas had finally gotten back together. Then she'd speculate about how long it would take Aaron to realize he was in love with her. Around midnight she noticed that Benjamin and Nina had been locked in Nina's room for a very long time.

*   *   *

Aisha and Christopher made out in Christopher's room. Both made a conscious effort to avoid the subject of marriage and focus on kissing instead. Aisha finally left when Christopher started pushing her to "go a little further."

Jake and Lara celebrated the first night of Jake's Christmas break with a bottle of Jagermeister. When Jake asked Lara where she kept getting the alcohol, she was evasive.

Lucas started to walk to Zoey's house three times. Each time he turned around before he got to her front yard. He went over a fourth time and got close enough to the house to peer up at her window and wonder if Aaron was inside. He decided he'd better not investigate.

Zoey almost called Lucas five times. She also almost called Aaron five times. Once, she walked out the front door with the intention of going to Lucas's. She got only as far as the driveway, where she was disturbed to hear shrieks of male and female laughter coming from Lara's room. Another time she left the house planning to go see Aaron. She was halfway up the block before she decided that was a very bad idea.

Before she went to bed Zoey wrote a poem about Lucas. She thought about submitting it to the Weymouth High literary magazine but tore it up instead. As she was falling asleep she decided she'd have a slumber party the next night. She was badly in need of female bonding, and besides, it would take her mind off Lucas (and Aaron).

Eleven

"I can't believe I let you guys talk me into this," Claire said.

It was eight o'clock on Saturday evening. Zoey, Nina, Aisha, and Claire were gathered in the Passmores' living room, where they were in stage one of the slumber party.

"You didn't have to come, Claire," Aisha pointed out.

"In fact, we would have preferred that you stayed home," Nina added. She thought for a moment. "Although that would have given you more time to perfect your hexes."

"Nina, you crack me up," Claire said dryly.

Zoey stood in the center of the room and waved her hands. "No sibling rivalry tonight, please, amusing as it is."

Nina rolled her eyes. She wasn't sure she could be in a room with her disgustingly perfect sister for over a minute without experiencing sibling rivalry. But she smiled sweetly. "Cross my heart. No more remarks about Claire's skill in the dark arts."

"And I won't mention Nina's flat chest once," Claire added.

Zoey stamped her foot. "We are now going to

watch *It's a Wonderful Life*. We will then go to my bedroom, where we will discuss anything but men.''

"What else is there to talk about?" Aisha asked.

Nina observed that Zoey glared—almost snarled—at Aisha. "Tonight is about women. Not men. Now everyone shut up so we can all be moved by the touching story of George Bailey."

Nina leaned back on the couch, preparing herself for the two hours of boredom she had to go through once a year with Zoey. *It's a Wonderful Life* was an outdated tradition, in her opinion. All in all, she'd rather be going for time number three with Benjamin.

"What time is Benjamin coming home?" Nina asked suddenly. Benjamin had been banished to Christopher's, where the guys were supposedly discussing cars and sports teams.

Zoey pushed the mute button. "First of all, I'm not my brother's keeper. Second of all, you are not going to hang out with Benjamin tonight. You promised."

"You mean there's not going to be a panty raid?" Nina pouted. "That's what happened at slumber parties on *Happy Days*."

Zoey rolled her eyes. "Nina, I'm warning you. . . ."

"Yes, sir." Nina saluted.

After Zoey turned the sound back on, Claire leaned toward Nina. "Is it my imagination, or has Zoey lost her mind?"

Nina didn't say anything. As happened once in a long while, she agreed with Claire.

*   *   *

By midnight, Claire had begun to question her judgment in agreeing to participate in Zoey's junior-high-throwback slumber party. She'd assumed that Zoey would eventually break down and reveal her latest love triangle—Zoey wasn't known for being introverted when it came to matters of the heart.

But they'd moved from the living room to Zoey's bedroom almost two hours before, and so far Claire had been bored stiff. Since they'd heard Benjamin come home thirty minutes earlier, Nina kept staring mournfully at the door. Zoey had managed to keep all discussion centered around clothes, exams, and her dislike of Lara McAvoy.

"I'm going downstairs to get a diet Coke," Aisha announced. "Anybody want one?"

"Hey, I'll go, Eesh," Nina offered.

"No, you won't," Zoey ordered. "And yes, I do want a diet Coke."

"I'll take a Dr Pepper," Nina said, sounding resentful.

Aisha left the room, and Zoey resumed the analysis of her history exam. "I mean, I know we studied Jamestown, but that's, like, so unimportant compared to World War Two."

"No offense, Zo, but who cares?" Nina interrupted. "Exams are over. Enjoy your freedom."

"I suppose you'd rather talk about making sheep eyes at Benjamin," Zoey said.

"Nope." Nina stood up. "I'm going to paint my toenails. Aisha said she brought some purple nail polish." Nina pushed herself off the bed and headed toward Aisha's overnight bag.

"Oh, goody," Claire said. "Maybe one of you will do my hair."

"What's this?" Nina asked. She'd been rummaging through Aisha's bag, but instead of retrieving the polish, she'd pulled out a small black box.

Aisha walked into the room holding three cans of soda. "Nothing," she yelled. "It's nothing."

Claire raised an eyebrow. She watched with interest as Nina snapped open the box. "A ring," she announced.

Aisha threw the cans she was holding to Zoey and rushed forward. She grabbed the box from Nina. "Do you mind?"

"Jeez, Eesh, why are you so hot and bothered?" Nina asked.

Aisha shoved the box into the pocket of her jeans. "I'm not!"

Claire noticed that Zoey was being awfully quiet. However, she looked entirely alert. Something was up.

"Man, you'd think it was, like, an *engagement* ring or something," Nina muttered. "I was just looking at the dumb thing."

Aisha's dark skin turned slightly ashen. "It is," she said quietly.

Claire stared at Aisha. Nina stared at Aisha. Zoey stared at the floor. "Oh, man," Nina cried. "This is wild!"

"Not to mention absurd," Claire added.

"Save us the editorial comments, Claire," Zoey snapped. "Aisha's confused enough as it is."

"Zoey, you actually *knew* that Christopher had popped the big question, and you didn't *tell* me?" Nina shrieked. She sank to the floor.

"Calm down, Nina," Aisha said. "I was going to keep the whole thing a secret, but the subject of commitment sort of naturally came up when Zoey was talking about how she fooled around with Aaron.''

Claire smiled to herself. At last the truth was out. Now Claire could sit back and relax. There was no way the night would end without Zoey agonizing over what she should do about her love life. Claire would wait for just the right moment, then chime in with her seemingly objective opinion. Perfect.

Nina gasped, then reached for her backpack. ''You and Aaron? When? Where? How? And most important, why didn't I know about it?'' She grabbed a new pack of Lucky Strikes from her bag.

''You've kind of been in your own world lately,'' Zoey pointed out. ''I would have told you the other day, but you wanted to hang out with Benjamin instead of with Eesh and me.''

Nina pulled out a cigarette. ''Well, things with Benjamin have been kind of . . . intense lately.''

''We know, Nina,'' Zoey said. ''You're scared that Benjamin's going to get his sight back and things won't be the same between you two.''

''It's not just that. . . .'' Nina sucked hard on the Lucky Strike. Claire noticed that her eyes were darting all around the room.

''If you guys were any more lovey-dovey than you already are, I might not be able to hold down food,'' Zoey interrupted.

''This from the girl who's been known to feed her boyfriend french fries in the lunchroom?'' Nina demanded.

As Claire observed the rising color on Nina's cheeks, a crazy, unbelievable thought occurred to her. She decided to take a stab. ''What Nina's trying to tell you all, in her own bumbling way, is that she and Benjamin finally did the dirty deed.''

91

"You had sex?" Zoey yelled. "With my brother?"

"Hey, how did you know?" Nina hollered, glaring at Claire.

Claire flashed her coolest, most self-satisfied smile. "I didn't. Until now, that is."

"I can't believe you and Benjamin *did* it," Zoey yelled again.

"Shut up, will you?" Nina whispered. "The whole neighborhood doesn't need to know about my private life."

"Just the whole house." Lara had appeared at Zoey's bedroom door.

"Oh, man, can Benjamin, like, hear what we're saying?" Nina sucked even harder on her cigarette.

"No, but I think Darla might be digging for her safe sex pamphlets," Lara answered.

Aisha giggled. "The horror, the horror."

"Great. Now my mom's going to think that *I'm* having sex, too," Zoey moaned. "She'll probably slip condoms into my pile of clean laundry."

"Are you?" Nina asked.

"Am I what?"

"Duh. Having sex."

"No!" Zoey huffed indignantly. "Unlike some people, I would tell my best friends if I lost my virginity."

Aisha removed the velvet box from her pocket and pulled out the ring for everyone to see. "Excuse me, but I think the fact that Christopher proposed to me is a little more important than Nina's losing her virginity."

"Hey, you only lose your virginity once. Who knows how many times you might be proposed to?" Nina said testily.

"Uh, do you want to join us, Lara?" Aisha asked.

"Gee, I've never been to a Girl Scout meeting before," Lara said.

"I guess you were too busy helping the Boy Scouts earn their badges," Claire said in her iciest voice.

Lara smirked. "Well, right now I'm helping a Boy Scout named Jake. So if you'll excuse me . . ." She backed out of the room and let the door slam behind her.

"She was drunk," Zoey commented.

"Definitely," Claire agreed.

Zoey threw a pillow at the door. "I swear, that girl is trying to re-create my life," she said.

"What do you mean?" Aisha asked.

"Isn't it obvious? She moved into my house, she's been working at the restaurant, and now she's going out with my old boyfriend."

"You're extremely paranoid, Zoey," Claire said.

Aisha nodded. "Let's not worry about Lara. I want to hear more about Nina's burgeoning sex life." She turned to Nina. "So, are you going to do anything about birth control?"

"What do you mean?" Nina asked. She tossed her chewed-up cigarette in the trash and reached for a fresh one.

"Nina, please tell me that you and Benjamin didn't use the old no-one-gets-pregnant-the-first-time philosophy." Claire made her voice as condescending as possible. She knew Nina had the impression that Claire was well versed in sex, and she intended to keep it that way.

"Last time I checked, I *did* have a brain, Claire. We used a thingy."

"A thingy?" Aisha said.

"Fine. A *condom*, if you insist on being graphic about it."

"You should go on the Pill," Claire said, just to see Nina's reaction.

Claire was gratified to see that Nina looked as if she wanted to crawl under Zoey's bed. "I thought all those hormones were dangerous for smokers."

"You don't smoke, Nina," Zoey pointed out. "You suck on unlit pieces of tobacco-filled paper."

"Still . . ."

"Condoms can break," Aisha pointed out.

"Can we just stop this conversation right now?" Nina yelled.

Good call, little sister, Claire said silently. Now she just had to wait for them to wade through the topic of Christopher's proposal. After that, they'd inevitably work their way back to the most interesting topic up for discussion—what Zoey was going to do about Lucas.

Nina

on the question of the Question

According to the AP bulletin, otherwise known as the Chatham Island gossip mill, Christopher Shupe has popped the question. Recipient of that popping was Aisha Gray, who next to Zoey is my best friend.

The obvious follow-up inquiry is...drum roll, please...what will the answer be?

There are several reasons Aisha might decide to say yes. For one thing, she's in love with Christopher. And it appears that he's in love with her, given the fact that he just asked her, in effect, to be (1) the woman to run up all of his credit cards to the max once he gets rich, goes through a midlife crisis, and has an affair with his secretary, (2) the woman who goes through incredible pain in order to bear his children, and (3) the woman who laughs at him when he gets really old and has to keep his teeth in a glass of cleaning solution every night.

So they've got the love thing going on. And let's face it, marriage offers some security. I mean, what if Benjamin regains his sight, decides I'm about as attractive as a female version of Henry Kissinger, and dumps me? All

I can do is beg and plead for him to see my inner beauty, then spend the rest of my life a bitter and lonely woman.

If we were married, he'd have to accept me no matter what. Unless, of course, he decided to get a divorce. In that event, I'd have huge lawyer bills and I'd be bitter and lonely. Have I just undermined my own argument? I'm losing track.

Anyway, if Christopher goes into the army without anything to keep him tied to Aisha, he'll probably end up forgetting her. Sort of like the way Benjamin will maybe forget me if he gets his sight back and decides to

travel around the world on a
whirlwind adventure.

And knowing Aisha, she'll
probably end up forgetting
Christopher. Or at least making
herself forget him. She's very
rational that way. (Unlike me,
who would pine away until I was
nothing but an old flannel shirt
and a pair of Doc Martens.)

And the thought of those two
forgetting about each other, for
no better reason than the idiotic
United States Army, seems like a
conspiracy on the scale of who
really shot JFK.

The darker side of their getting
married is that I'd probably have
to be a bridesmaid. Which means

I'd have to wear a really ugly dress that would then rot in the back of my closet for the next fifty years. If there's one thing I'm certain of in this world, it's that I do not look good in fuchsia taffeta. Does anyone?

Claire

on the matter of the Proposal

Should Christopher and Aisha get
married? They've got to be joking. It's
the worst idea I've ever heard.

First of all, Christopher's eyes seem
to have a will of their own. Despite the
fact that Aisha claims the guy has broken
his habit of getting a little something on the
side, I've seen him examine my legs
as if they were two of the seven
wonders of the world.

Second, Aisha is totally immature. She
seems to have the misguided notion that
being good at math and science
automatically makes her a rational,
pragmatic person. In fact, she's a
hopeless romantic (even worse than

Zoey) trapped in the body of a college-bound honors student.

Oh, yes. College. Aisha's insane if she thinks she'll really finish school once she and Christopher get married. She'll end up getting pregnant, abandoning her education, and having to make a fulfilling career out of baking cookies and knitting booties.

I give the marriage five years. Just enough time for Aisha to get saddled with three screaming toddlers and a mortgage payment.

Of course, I'm going to keep these opinions to myself. What Aisha does is entirely her business. Sure, I might make a subtle suggestion here and there, but I won't say anything that anyone

could call an opinion. I'll just ask a
few choice questions.

I do hope that, if this farce comes to
fruition, I won't be forced to be a
bridesmaid. I can think of little that would
be more demeaning than parading down
the aisle of a church wearing an aqua
faux silk dress and knowing all the time
that Aisha was throwing her life straight
into the trash.

BENJAMIN

pondering possible impending nuptials

Should Aisha marry Christopher?
Let me think about that question for
about one second. Okay. Got it. The
answer is a definite, resounding no.

All of us live on this tiny island,
virtually isolated from the rest of the
known world. We go about our
everyday business as if we were
never going to leave Chatham Island.
I mean, Zoey kisses a guy who isn't
her boyfriend, and suddenly our
world is shattered into a million
pieces. In other words, our
perspective is more than a little
skewed.

Someday we're all going to leave
Chatham, at least for college.
Personally, I'd like to travel around
the world and experience a thousand
different cultures. Sure, I love Nina. I
may even want to marry her
someday. But does that mean I'm
going to make that kind of decision
now, when I've never even been to
California?

But of course, I'm different from everybody else. If this surgery doesn't create a miracle, then I have to face the hard fact that my options are limited.

LUCAS

on consummation
(And — oh, yeah — love)

If the only way for me to
have sex with Zoey was to
marry her, then I would do it
in a second. I'm in love with
her, and I'm sure that I will
be for the rest of my life.

At least I was sure, until
I caught her in a heavy lip lock
with Aaron. (Is it just me, or
is Aaron a majorly wussy name for
a guy?) Now I don't know if
Zoey's even officially my
girlfriend anymore.

Even beyond the whole living-
as-husband-and-wife part of
marriage, I understand
Christopher's wanting to get
Aisha to say "I do." Guys have
this natural territorial
instinct. Sort of like dogs who
pee on something to establish
that it's theirs.

I mean, when I see another

guy look At Zoey (AAron, for instance), I wAnt to punch him until he's just A quivering mass of blood And guts. Then I wAnt to put A little sign Around Zoey's neck to indicAte thAt she's mine. A tAttoo Across her foreheAd would be even better.

Now thAt Christopher's leAving the islAnd to join the Army, he wAnts to mAke sure AishA's not going to strAy. There's only one problem: whether or not people love you hAs nothing to do with pieces of pAper or wedding rings or even solemn vows.

Love is more About pretending not to notice A zit on your girlfriend's cheek or Admitting to her thAt you're terrified your life will Amount to nothing. It's About not Accusing her of hAving PMS every time she gets mAd At you. Love is listening And trusting And deciding in eAch of your minds thAt you're willing to make this messy thing called a relationship work.

Most of all, love is about accepting disappointment. I know I'm in love with Zoey, because I'm willing to forgive her fooling around with Aaron. (The way she forgave me for doing the same thing with Claire.)

In other words, I have no idea whether or not Christopher and Aisha should get married.

If they do decide to hold their noses and take the plunge, I wouldn't mind seeing Zoey as a bridesmaid. I remember from the one wedding I went to, when I was thirteen, that girls look great in those flowery, pastel dresses.

JAKE

Marriage is a big step. I
guess any idiot knows that
much. For a long, long time
there was no doubt in my mind
that Zoey and I would get
married. Then she dumped me
for Lucas, and the whole idea
of us living happily ever after
sort of blew up in my face.

In general, I'm promarriage.
A lot of people think I'm just
a dumb jock who doesn't have
any philosophy of life beyond
"catch the ball and keep
running." But I think about
life, not to mention death, all
the time. Wade's death

taught me that love and relationships are the most important things in life. If I had a wife and kids, I'd treat them with complete respect and loyalty.

At least, I hope I would. When I look at my dad, I realize that seemingly good people can be pretty scummy at times. My dad cheats on my mom, and the whole island knows about it.

Christopher and Aisha seem to really be in love. Then again, I thought Zoey and I were in love. I even thought Claire and I were in love for the five seconds that we were actually going out. Lara and I...well, that's another story. We're something, but I don't think it's "in love."

Anyway, Christopher and Aisha. I don't know. I guess I'm not close enough to either one to say whether or not they could stand each other for another fifty years. I just hope they know what they're doing.

If they do get married, the wedding will really be something. Aisha will be the first island kid to get married. All of us guys will probably have to go into Portland and rent tuxes. And the girls will wear those long, flowing dresses. All matching. That'll be nice. Maybe. I'll even get to dance with Zoey.

Zoey

Marriage? Under normal circumstances, I could wax poetic about this topic forever. But life is no longer normal, and I'm in absolutely no position to discuss someone else's relationship. I can't even keep my own in a decent condition.

But I will say this: Aisha is in love with Christopher. That's a fact. I am in love with Lucas. That is (or was) a fact. Yet I, Zoey Passmore, a usually upstanding citizen, found myself irresistibly drawn to another guy. I then allowed myself to make out with that guy. Yet one more fact.

If I could do something like

that, who's to say that Aisha
won't? Or Christopher?
Especially Christopher. It's
one of those things where if
A equals B, then C is also
possible.

The thing is, all of us are at
a stage in our lives where
we're constantly changing.
And we never know what's
around the next corner. I
mean, if someone had told me a
year ago that Benjamin might
be able to see again someday,
or that Nina would no longer
be a virgin, or that I would
have a half sister, I would
have laughed in their face.

I guess what I've learned
in the past few weeks is that
none of us really knows
anything. We're just
bumbling through life,
trying our best to manage
what comes our way.

And I'm not sure any of

us, including Christopher and Aisha, should made a decision that's, like, irreversible (divorce aside).

Then again, since I don't know anything, I shouldn't be telling other people how they should live their lives. In other words, I'm going to keep my mouth shut.

If Aisha does get married, I hope I get to help pick out the bridesmaids dresses. I've always wanted to be a bridesmaid...

Twelve

Saturday afternoon Aisha circled the parking lot of the Weymouth Mall for the third time. The huge structure was surrounded by thousands of parking spaces, and every single one was filled. Aisha honked the horn of her parents' Taurus at a harried-looking woman who didn't seem to realize that Aisha was waiting to move down the lane.

"I feel like I'm in purgatory," Nina said.

"It's more like hell," Zoey countered.

Aisha honked again. "I can't believe I let you guys talk me into this."

"Eesh, there's no *way* you finished all of your Christmas shopping already," Nina said.

Aisha raised an eyebrow. "Unlike you procrastinators, I planned ahead. Remember the day after Thanksgiving? While you guys were stocking up on books and CDs for yourself, I was shopping for loved ones."

"Does it sound like she's saying 'I told you so'?" Nina asked Zoey.

Zoey was riding shotgun. She turned to face Nina. "A definite 'I told you so.' She's enjoying our misery."

"I'm not enjoying anything. Thanks to you guys,

114

I've got to suffer these crowds like a commoner.''

Over eggs and pancakes that morning, Nina and Zoey had decided it was imperative that they go to the mall to do their Christmas shopping. Unfortunately, Mrs. Passmore was using the family van to pick up supplies for the restaurant. Nina had then called home, only to find out that Claire had already taken the ferry to Weymouth, where she planned to take out the Geigers' Mercedes.

"Claire *knew* I wanted to go to the mall today," Nina said. "That's why she sneaked out of Zoey's so early—so she could take the car for herself."

"That's Claire for you," Aisha commented.

"And I have to buy the witch a Christmas present. Where is the justice?"

Zoey reached back and patted Nina's head. "Now, now, Claire *was* on her best behavior last night."

"You're just saying that because she gave you advice about how to get back together with Lucas," Nina said.

Aisha spotted a parking space on the other side of the lot. She pressed the gas pedal and gunned the car at a dangerous speed toward the rectangle of concrete.

"Whatever." Zoey turned back around.

"So, what did you get Christopher?" Nina asked Aisha. "I have, like, less than no idea what I should get for Benjamin."

Aisha smiled to herself. On her way home from Zoey's that morning, she'd noticed a broken-down island car sitting in front of the house of Mr. Hartley, one of Zoey's neighbors. As soon as she'd seen the For Sale sign in the window, she'd gone up and knocked on his door.

Fifteen minutes later, Aisha had shaken Mr. Hartley's hand. She'd gotten him to come down to $120 from his original $200 asking price. Aisha was going to drop the cash off the next afternoon, at which point she would become officially broke.

"Hello, Aisha? Anyone home?" Nina shouted from the backseat. "I said, what did you get your fiancé for Christmas?"

Aisha pulled triumphantly into the parking space. "First of all, he's not my fiancé—yet. Second of all, it's none of your business. It's a surprise."

Nina groaned. "I'm doomed. I'm going to end up getting Benjamin some really dorky shirt or a bottle of cheesy cologne."

"You think you've got problems," Zoey said, unbuckling her seat belt. "I still haven't decided if I should even get Lucas a present." She paused. "As for Aaron . . ."

Aisha sighed as she set the parking brake. It was going to be one bad day at the mall.

Claire ducked quickly behind a rack of clothes in The Gap. She'd just spotted Nina, Zoey, and Aisha heading into the store, and she had no desire to get bitched out by Nina for taking the car for herself.

Claire found that shopping in groups was both annoying and inefficient. With other people, there was the inevitable waiting around for someone to try stuff on. Plus she had to constantly comment on whether or not so-and-so would like such-and-such, and there was always stop after stop at the women's room.

Alone, Claire could whip through stores at her own pace. In the past hour and a half, for instance, she'd gotten presents for her dad, Nina, and Sarah.

116

The only person left on her list was Aaron.

Claire had already considered, then rejected, a dozen different gift ideas. Aaron, she'd discovered, was not easy to shop for. Silk boxers were too obvious, a fisherman's sweater too boring, a book too pretentious. She'd almost purchased a beautiful fedora, but she'd put her American Express card away at the last second. A person's taste in hats was almost impossible to predict.

Standing by the mirrored wall at the back of the store, Claire saw Nina, Aisha, and Zoey walking toward a display of turtlenecks. She seized the moment to make her getaway.

Outside The Gap, Claire headed for the escalator. A small antiques store on the second floor of the mall was her last hope. If she didn't find a gift for Aaron there, she'd have to settle for wrapping a bow around her head and offering herself up as a present. Actually, that wasn't a terrible idea.

Who bought whom what for Christmas: THE GIRLS

Zoey

For Mrs. Passmore: one silk scarf, marked down, from Banana Republic

For Mr. Passmore: one Jerry Garcia's Last Tour tie-dyed, long-sleeved T-shirt, from House of Groove

For Benjamin: the collected works of Robert Johnson, from Musicland

For Lara: one conservative white blouse, marked down, from The Gap

For Lucas: one leather wallet, with his initials stamped in gold, from the Jones Store

For Aaron (against her better judgment): one *Best of the Blues* songbook, from Musicland

Nina

For Mr. Geiger: one wallet just like the one Zoey bought, only with her dad's initials instead of Lu-

cas's, plus one bottle of Brut cologne, from the
Jones Store

For Claire: one bottle of Chanel nail polish and
matching lipstick, from the Jones Store

For Sarah: one bowl of potpourri, from Home and
Hearth

For Aaron: one T-shirt with the word *Stud* written
across the front, from T-shirt Mania

For Benjamin: one silk robe, from Brooks Brothers,
and one Nine Inch Nails poster (which she
planned to say was a photograph of the Grand
Canyon), from Musicland

Claire

For Mr. Geiger: one Hermés tie, from Brooks Brothers, and one box of gold-tipped fireplace matches,
from Hearth and Home

For Nina: one Zippo lighter, minus the butane, from
House of Groove

For Sarah: one silk scarf, from Banana Republic

For Aaron: one antique wooden cigar box, ornately
carved, from Relics from the Past

Aisha

For Mrs. Gray: one cookbook by Martha Stewart,
from B. Dalton

For Mr. Gray: one hardback edition of *The Ency-
clopedia of Maine and Other Great States*,
marked down, from B. Dalton

For Kalif: one miniature Nerf basketball and hoop, from Sports Sensation
For Christopher: one seriously hurting island car, from old Mr. Hartley on Bristol Street

Thirteen

"No offense, Benjamin, but can we, like, take a handicapped space since you're in the car?" Jake asked Monday afternoon. He was growing increasingly frustrated by the lack of parking spaces in the enormous lot at the Weymouth Mall.

"Oh, sure, Jake. I'll just pull out the handy Crippled sign I keep in my back pocket. You can hang it over the rearview mirror."

Jake grimaced. "Never mind."

In the backseat, Lucas muttered an expletive.

"Hey, I'm the one doing you a favor here, Cabral," Jake said. "Lay off."

"Someone's pulling out of a space in front of the Jones Store," Christopher called from the backseat.

Jake nodded and headed the Honda toward the spot. He hoped the rest of the day wouldn't be as trying as the last hour had been. When Benjamin had called and explained that he, Lucas, and Christopher were all in desperate need of transportation to the Weymouth Mall, Jake had reluctantly offered his services. Hanging out with Lucas wasn't number one on his list of fun ways to spend Christmas vacation, but since Jake had been planning to do some last-minute Christmas shopping himself, he hadn't felt there was any honorable way to get out of carpool duty.

But as soon as they'd gotten on the ferry, Lucas had started to give him attitude. Apparently things between Lucas and Zoey were pretty bad and he felt the need to take it out on Zoey's ex. Jake had pointed out that if Lucas hadn't stolen Zoey in the first place, he wouldn't be having problems now. Finally Benjamin had tried to intervene, which had made the atmosphere even tenser.

"I feel like a girl," Lucas said as Jake pulled into the free parking space. "Girls are always going to the mall in big, giggling groups."

"It's not like we do this every day," Christopher said. "Christmas is just one of those times when everyone has to suck it up and head for the stores."

"What're you getting Aisha?" Jake asked. He'd been debating what to get Lara for days, but the only items he'd thought of were sexy lingerie and a bottle of liquor.

Unfortunately, he wouldn't be caught dead in a women's underwear store, and he'd thrown away Wade's old ID, which he'd always used to buy alcohol, when he'd gone on the wagon a few weeks before. Talk about a stupid move.

"I already gave it to her," Christopher answered. "I'm just going to get her something small today."

"So what *did* you get?" Jake asked.

"Uh, a ring."

"A ring?"

"Man, does he have to spell it out?" Lucas snapped. "He got her a damn engagement ring."

"Oh." Jake didn't know what to say.

Christopher unbuckled his seat belt and climbed

out of the car. "Gee, Lucas, thanks for keeping my business *my business*."

Lucas got out of the other side of the car. "Chill out, Christopher. Everybody already knows."

Benjamin nodded. "I wasn't going to say anything to Zoey about it after you told me Saturday night, but it turned out that Aisha spilled the news at Zoey's slumber party anyway."

"Man, this is wild," Jake said. "What did she say?"

Christopher glared at Jake. "She hasn't given me an answer yet, but she's going to say yes."

Jake shook his head. A few months before, he'd thought that he and Zoey would get married and that Claire and Benjamin probably would as well. Aisha and Christopher hadn't been an official couple. They hadn't even had a date. Now Benjamin and Jake were with different people, and Aisha and Christopher were getting ready to head down the aisle.

Life was crazy. So crazy that he felt he could use a drink. Maybe two.

Who bought whom what for Christmas: THE GUYS

BENJAMIN

For Mrs. Passmore: one pair dangly earrings (supposedly silver and copper), from Natural Wear

For Mr. Passmore: one pair John Lennon–style sunglasses, from House of Groove

For Zoey: one new journal, leather-bound, from B. Dalton

For Lara: one wall tapestry, marked down, from House of Groove

For Nina: one silver heart-shaped locket, from Just to Say I Love You, and one pack Lucky Strikes

LUCAS

For Mrs. Cabral: one sturdy apron, from Function Junction
For Mr. Cabral: one pair waterproof thermal gloves
For Zoey: one silver charm bracelet, from Just to Say I Love You

JAKE

For Mrs. McRoyan: one bottle of Ombré Rose perfume, from the Jones Store
For Mr. McRoyan: one subscription to *Time* magazine, with a sample issue, from Ernie's Newsstand
For Lara: one pair rhinestone earrings, from Just to Say I Love You

Christopher

For Mrs. Gray: one bottle of scented hand lotion, from the Jones Store
For Mr. Gray: one paperback book called *Crime and the Inner City*, from B. Dalton
For Kalif: one Yankees baseball cap, from Sports Sensation
For Aisha: one silver barrette, from The Gap

Fourteen

"On the first day of Christmas my true love gave to me . . . ," Christopher sang as he walked up the path to Gray House Tuesday night. His voice trailed off. What would his true love give him for Christmas? An answer?

Aisha opened the door before he had a chance to ring the bell. "Merry Christmas Eve," she called.

"Same to you, and then some." Christopher felt a sharp pang of desire as his eyes drank in the sight of Aisha.

She was already dressed for the Grays' party, and she looked incredible. Her short red dress set off her dark skin, while her upswept hair highlighted her high cheekbones. She was even wearing his favorite bright red lipstick. Before he could lean forward to kiss her, she darted out of the house.

"What are you doing?" he asked. "You'll freeze."

She clasped his arm. "This'll just take a minute. Besides, you'll keep me warm."

Christopher put his arm around her, and she led him across the grass toward the side of the house. "Where are we going?"

She laughed. "Be patient."

Christopher's heart pounded. Maybe this was it. Maybe she wanted to be alone with him so that she could say yes. He nodded to himself. That had to be it. She wouldn't look so happy if she was going to refuse his offer of marriage. It would be too cruel, even for a girl.

Aisha pulled him to a stop at the top of Climbing Way, the road that led to her house. "Ta-da!" she cried.

He looked around but saw nothing remarkable. "What?"

She hugged him around the waist, beaming. "Merry Christmas."

"Eesh, I think I'm missing something here."

She stood on her tiptoes and gave him a kiss on the cheek. "I'm giving you your Christmas present, silly."

Christopher grinned. "And it's you?"

She giggled again. "No, it's over there." She pointed to the road.

All Christopher saw was a beat-up island car. "I still don't get it."

"Christopher, look closely at that car."

As he walked to the car, he saw that someone had placed a huge red bow on its somewhat dented roof. "You're giving me a car?" he asked, incredulous.

She grinned. "I can't have my boyfriend freezing his butt off every morning." She opened the passenger door of the car. "There's no backseat and no radio, *but* the heat works."

"Aisha, you shouldn't have. . . ."

She shrugged and slid into the car. "Hey, Christmas is the season of giving to the ones you love. Besides, Mr. Hartley gave me a great deal."

He ran around to the driver's side and hopped in.

When he'd shut the door, Aisha handed him the keys. "Let's check out the heater."

"Last time we did this, your mom had a fit," Christopher reminded her.

"Yes, but that was at four o'clock in the morning."

He laughed at the memory. "Good point."

As they waited for the car to warm up, Christopher took Aisha's hands in his. "I love the present, Aisha."

She raised an eyebrow. "You don't sound very convincing. What, you expected a Porsche?"

He shook his head. "It's just that I'm not going to have a lot of time to use it."

She narrowed her eyes, frowning. "What . . . what do you mean?" Her voice was high and slightly shrill.

"I need an answer, Eesh. Soon."

She pulled her hands away and crossed her arms in front of her chest. "What are you saying?" she whispered.

"I got a call from Lieutenant Lang today," Christopher began.

Aisha shook her head vigorously from side to side. "No, Christopher, no."

He tried to take her hand again, but she flinched when he touched her. "I ship out on January fifth," he said softly.

Aisha banged the sagging dashboard of the car with her fists. "No! I said no!"

"Aisha . . ."

She suddenly turned and threw herself into his arms. Immediately he felt the moisture of her tears through his cotton shirt. "I'm sorry, baby," he said soothingly.

She hiccuped, then pulled away so she could look at him. "But Christopher, I still don't know what to say. I don't know what's best."

He tucked a stray curl behind her ear and brushed a tear from her cheek. "Say yes, Eesh. We can leave together. We can be together forever."

She leaned forward again, pressing her head against his shoulder. "I need more time. I haven't even told my parents. . . ."

He couldn't stand her tears or the agonizing pain in her voice. Christopher rubbed his hand up and down her back, trying to soothe her. "Don't worry, Aisha. Don't worry. . . ."

But Christopher was worried. If Aisha didn't make up her mind before January fifth to marry him, he was going to lose her. And he didn't think he could stand a life without Aisha Gray by his side.

Lucas threaded his way through the crowd of Chatham Island residents in order to follow Zoey. He almost hadn't come to Gray House for fear that Zoey and Aaron might be there together, but at the last minute he'd changed his mind. He wasn't going to lose her without at least trying to work things out. The roll-over-and-die strategy was simply not in his best interests.

Aaron Mendel had been out of sight since Lucas had walked into the party, but Lucas had kept his eyes glued on Zoey. Now he could no longer keep himself away. At this point he didn't care who'd done what to whom. He just wanted her back.

He caught sight of her again just as she walked into the Grays' first-floor bathroom. Lucas leaned against the wall of the narrow hallway leading to the bathroom to wait. *Be cool*, he reminded himself. He had to play this moment right.

When Zoey emerged, Lucas stepped out of the shadows. She gasped. "It's just me," he said quietly.

She continued forward until they were face-to-face, then stopped. "I've missed you," Lucas whispered.

"Oh, Lucas. I've missed you, too."

Lucas walked toward Zoey, forcing her to back up against the wall. He placed his hands against the wall at either side of her waist, effectively trapping her within his arms.

"How much?" he asked in his sexiest voice.

He saw her swallow hard. Her lips trembled slightly. "A lot."

He moved one hand so that he could lightly run his fingers down the side of her face. He allowed his thumb to rest on her soft, red lips. "What've you missed?"

Her eyes seemed glued to his. "Kissing you."

Lucas leaned forward and covered Zoey's mouth with his. Relief flooded through his body. At last he was kissing Zoey again. After almost a minute, he pulled away.

"Can we try again?" he asked.

"Oh, Lucas . . ." Zoey hugged him close.

Lucas murmured her name over and over. They were meant to be together. He was sure of that now. "I love—"

He broke off when he felt Zoey stiffen in his arms. For a moment he was confused. Had he been hugging her too tightly? It was possible, considering that he was making up for over a week of not being able to touch her at all. Then he saw that her gaze was fixed just over his shoulder.

Lucas turned and found himself staring straight at Aaron Mendel. "What the hell—"

"Hello, Lucas," Aaron said evenly. "Zoey."

Zoey's gaze darted from Lucas to Aaron. She looked like a trapped animal.

"Get the hell away from us!" Lucas shouted. A wave of pure rage swept through him.

"Lucas!" Zoey cried.

Aaron held up a hand. "Hey, I understand."

Lucas stepped away and grabbed Aaron by his silk tie. "No, I don't think you do, pretty boy."

From what seemed a mile away, Lucas heard Zoey pleading for him to let Aaron loose. But Lucas was powerless against his anger. At that moment he wanted nothing more than to knock Aaron unconscious.

"Yes, I'm considering both Harvard and MIT," Claire said to Mr. Gray. She'd been stuck talking to Aisha's dad for the past fifteen minutes, and her smile felt as if it were about to break off her face.

"Great schools, but Boston can be a dangerous city," Mr. Gray said.

Claire nodded absently. "Yes, well . . ."

"Then again, Boston is a cultural center—"

"Excuse me, Mr. Gray," Claire interrupted. "I see someone I have to talk to."

Aaron had just walked by, and Claire wasn't going to let him get away. For the past hour he'd been talking to every adult in sight, mixing and mingling as if he were a diplomat. Unfortunately, he hadn't stopped to speak with Mr. Gray, the way she'd hoped.

"Nice talking with you, Claire," she heard Mr. Gray say as she took off in the direction of the first-floor bathroom.

As she passed the windows of the living room, Claire's eyes lit up. Outside, a light snow had started to fall. Finally things were going her way.

Claire walked purposefully, making sure not to make eye contact with anyone in her path. The last thing she needed was to get cornered by another well-meaning parent. Discussing plans for the future wasn't nearly as interesting as creating an exciting present.

Claire stopped at the front of the narrow hall that led to the bathroom. She stifled an irritated sigh. Aaron was not alone. In fact, he was eye to eye with Lucas, who had him in a choke hold. Zoey was pulling pathetically at Lucas's sleeve, begging him to let go.

"Lucas, don't be a jackass," Claire said icily.

"Shut up, Claire. This doesn't concern you," Lucas answered.

"If you make a scene, all of Chatham Island is going to know you as the idiot who spoiled the Grays' Christmas gala," Claire pointed out.

"Lucas, please," Zoey begged.

Lucas released Aaron. "Are you all right, Aaron?" Zoey asked, sounding every bit the concerned girlfriend.

Aaron laughed. "Hey, no harm done." He stuck his hand out toward Lucas. "How about a truce?"

"You make me sick," Lucas said, his voice raspy. He turned to Zoey. "And so do you."

Zoey watched, her jaw open, as Lucas stomped down the hall. Claire sent a silent curse in Lucas's

132

direction. After all the groundwork she'd done at the slumber party to soften Zoey up toward him, he'd totally screwed up. Why was it that guys never knew when to cut their losses?

Fifteen

The party was thinning out by the time Benjamin pulled Nina close and whispered in her ear, "I want to take a tour of the house."

She giggled. "Oh, really?"

"Yeah, but you know us blind folks. We can't wander around unfamiliar places without the help of a sighted person."

"Just a second. I'll go get Jake. I'm sure he'd love to lend you his elbow."

"Ha, ha."

She slipped an arm around his waist. "You mean you didn't have Jake in mind as a tour guide?"

"No, I was imagining someone with a much higher voice. And a better figure."

"Not me?" she asked.

Benjamin imagined Nina batting her eyelashes and grinning. He nodded. "Just make sure the tour ends in an empty room. Preferably an empty room with a lock on its door."

"Benjamin Passmore, are you planning to seduce me?"

"Take me to the empty room and you'll find out."

Nina took his arm and began leading him in what

he thought was the direction of the staircase. "I do love surprises," she murmured.

Jake was feeling good. He'd discovered that Lara had a talent for pouring rum and Cokes on the sly. They'd each downed several. Now they were locked in the first-floor bathroom, making out. Jake hadn't had one thought all night about how depressing another Christmas without Wade would be.

"Good party, huh?" Jake asked when Lara pulled away to take a sip of her drink.

Lara nodded. "Aisha's mom is quite the little hostess."

"And there's lots of holiday *spirit*," Jake added.

Lara giggled. "Yeah, and we've had most of it ourselves."

Jake set down his glass next to the sink. "We should probably get back out to the party. Someone might be waiting for the bathroom."

Lara gave him a long, hard kiss. "Hey, I know a better party."

"Yeah? Where?"

She grinned. "At my place."

Jake imagined falling into Lara's bed and what would happen next. "Let's go."

She shook her head. "We need to go shopping first."

Jake laughed. "Nothing's open, babe."

"Not at a *store*, Jakie." Lara unlocked the door and opened it.

Jake followed Lara through the house, feeling slightly woozy. They stopped at the front hall closet to get their coats, then continued to the door of the kitchen. Lara peered inside. "Coast's clear," she whispered.

Jake watched as Lara darted into the kitchen, where a couple of cartons of liquor were sitting on the counter. She picked up a jug of wine and stuck it under her coat. Jake laughed, impressed by the bold move.

"*Now* we can get out of here," Lara said. While she headed out of the kitchen, Jake lingered for a moment. He hesitated, then grabbed a bottle of vodka. He'd keep this one for himself.

Aisha struggled to get Zoey's arms into the sleeves of her coat. All the adult guests had left the party ages ago, along with most of the kids. But Zoey had discovered that she loved eggnog, and Aisha hadn't been able to get her away from the bowl. Unfortunately, it had only recently dawned on Aisha that Zoey was well on her way to being very tipsy, if not out-and-out wasted.

"Time to go home, Zo," Aisha coaxed, pulling on the coat.

Zoey managed to slide her arms into the sleeves, and Aisha breathed a sigh of relief. Mission one accomplished.

"I want to go home with Lucas," Zoey announced.

"I don't think that's going to happen tonight, Zoey." Lucas had left an hour earlier, which Zoey should have known, considering that he left because of her.

"You're right. Lucas is mean. Let's go find Aaron."

Aisha groaned. "Zoey, that is *not* a good idea. You're going to bed."

She glanced into the next room, where Claire and Aaron had been cornered by Mrs. Gray. For once

Aisha was thankful that her mom had a tendency to babble endlessly after a glass of wine. Aisha could get Zoey out of the house without Mr. and Mrs. Gray realizing that she was tipsy.

Benjamin and Nina suddenly appeared at the bottom of the staircase. They looked guilty but not *too* guilty. Aisha sent up a silent prayer that they hadn't done It in her house. "Hey, guys," Nina called. "What's going on?"

Aisha turned to Benjamin. "Your sister tied one on, Benjamin."

He laughed. "No way. Zoey never drinks."

Aisha shrugged. "She seems to have discovered that she has a passion for eggnog. And I don't think she realized that the stuff is spiked with rum." She glanced at Zoey, who was now sprawled on the couch. "That is, she didn't realize it till the fifth or sixth glass."

"Wait, wait. I've got it," Zoey yelled from the couch.

"What?" Nina asked.

"I want Jake. He's my true love. I'm sure of that now."

"Jake is with Lara," Aisha reminded her.

Zoey looked sad for a moment, then she giggled. "Oh, well. I guess she can have my leftovers."

Christopher walked in the front door, lightly dusted with snowflakes. "The car's warmed up."

As soon as Aisha heard the word *car*, a knot formed in the pit of her stomach. All night she'd been trying to forget what Christopher had told her earlier, but the mention of his new old car brought the horrific moment rushing back.

"Great, a ride," Nina said.

Zoey swayed toward Christopher, still laughing at

whatever she'd found so funny while she was sitting on the couch. She gave Christopher a light punch on the arm. "Hey, you're not going to be Christopher Shupe much longer."

"I'm not?" he asked, raising an eyebrow in Aisha's direction.

She giggled. "Nope. You're gonna be Mr. Aisha Gray."

"Ignore her, Christopher," Nina called from the front hall closet. She pulled out her and Benjamin's coats. "Zoey knows not of what she speaks."

Aisha stomped over to Zoey. Her temper was about to explode, but she forced herself to remain calm. It wasn't *Zoey's* fault that she'd been incredibly stupid and ignorant and gotten herself plastered. It was just one of those things.

Then Aisha smelled Zoey's breath, which made her gag. "Maybe you should let her crawl home, Christopher. She's going to smell up your car." Aisha was only half joking.

"I think the car will survive," Christopher responded. Nina laughed, and Benjamin looked worried.

"Hey, I'm serious. This is the nineties. We women have equal rights," Zoey pronounced, and threw her arm around Aisha's shoulder. "Christopher and Aisha, sittin' in a tree, K-I-S-S-I-N-G," Zoey sang off-key. "First comes love, then comes *marriage*—"

"Zoey, shut up," Nina warned.

Zoey looked crushed. "I thought you were supposed to be my best friend."

"I am. That's why I'm telling you to shut your damn mouth and let Christopher carry your drunk self to his brand-new car."

"You really have a way with words," Christopher commented.

"Drunk?" Zoey shouted. "I'm not drunk. That's impossible."

"Zoey, you're drunk."

"I just had a little eggnog," Zoey explained. "And I-I-I-I will always love yoooouuu. . . ."

"Oh, man, now she's singing cheesy Whitney Houston tunes. This situation is more dire than I'd thought."

"I never realized Zoey was tone-deaf," Benjamin commented.

Aisha shoved Zoey out the front door. "The things you learn at a party."

Sixteen

Christmas morning Zoey awoke to the sound of her father yelling "Ho, ho, ho" at the top of his lungs. She groaned. Her head felt as if someone had stuffed it with a Brillo pad.

Her father's loud knock on the door sounded like someone banging a gong. "Get up, Zo! Santa came last night."

She rolled over, squinting against the bright light that streamed in the window. "I'll be right down, Dad. Just, uh, let me brush my teeth."

"Don't be long," he called. "Santa might switch the candy in your stocking for coal."

As Zoey listened to her father tromp down the stairs, she wondered why he had to choose this particular day to act like Ward Cleaver. The man went through 364 days of the year as a laid-back hippie, but every Christmas he got an acute attack of hokeyness. She was *not* in the mood.

Zoey dragged herself out of bed and walked to her mirror. What she saw was not pretty. "This, Zoey Passmore, is what's commonly known as a hangover."

She would never, ever drink another cup of eggnog. The stuff was lethal. It simply wasn't fair to put alcohol in something that tasted so good. Unsuspecting victims could end up like . . . well, like *her*.

Ten minutes later, Zoey had managed to wash her face, brush her teeth, put on her robe, and get downstairs. She'd even stopped in the kitchen and drunk an entire glass of orange juice. Perhaps Christmas could be salvaged after all.

Then she walked into the living room and saw Lara. She'd taken the seat closest to the fireplace and was lounging in the polka-dot pajamas Zoey hated. So much for salvaging Christmas.

Mr. Passmore rushed toward Zoey, his red Santa cap tilted precariously on his head. "Merry Christmas, Zo!" He crushed Zoey against his chest in a huge bear hug.

She felt the glass of orange juice she'd downed working its way back up. "Merry Christmas, Dad, Mom."

Benjamin walked into the room, already dressed in jeans and a black turtleneck. "Don't keep me in suspense. Did Santa show up this year?" he asked.

Mrs. Passmore handed Benjamin a cup of coffee and hugged him to her side. "He sure did. And after we find out what he's brought, your dad's got a whole day of activities planned."

Zoey collapsed on the couch. She'd been awake for less than half an hour, and already she felt as though she needed a nap. She closed her eyes, wondering when Christmas had turned into a chore.

Benjamin made a show of enjoying the process of opening his gifts, but his mind was a million miles away. Actually, a few hundred miles away. By the next night he'd be in Boston, preparing for the biggest day of his life. It was kind of hard to be excited about a new sweater.

Benjamin carefully unwrapped the gift Lara had placed in his hands, pasting on a bright smile. He felt the object, puzzled.

"It's a pen," Lara announced.

"Gee, thanks, Lara. I needed a new pen." Behind his dark glasses, he rolled his eyes.

"I wasn't sure what to get a blind person."

"Yeah, we're rather hard to shop for."

"But you know how people are always coming up to you and going, 'Hey, you got a pen?' This way you'll have one."

"No arguing with that logic." He was actually moved by Lara's attempt to fit in to the family. He realized he felt profoundly sorry for her—and ashamed of the fact that he hadn't done more to reach out to her. After all, she *was* his and Zoey's half sister.

"Jeff, your turn," Lara announced to Mr. Passmore. On the other side of the room, Benjamin heard his father unwrapping something.

"My, how nice. It's a . . ."

"An incense burner," Lara said. "I figured it was the kind of thing an old hippie would be into."

"It is. It is."

Benjamin felt Zoey sit down on the arm of the chair. "You know, I should have gotten her a flask," she whispered.

Benjamin sighed. So much for blossoming familial ties. He'd be better off obsessing about the surgery.

Claire lounged on the Geigers' living room couch. She'd allowed her silk robe to fall open just enough to expose her bare leg to Aaron. In the last minute she'd seen his eyes travel to her calf at least six times. Progress.

They'd finally finished the tedious business of opening presents. Sarah had oohed and aahed over her gifts as if she'd never seen a bowl of potpourri or a scarf before. Of course, the gold-and-ruby bracelet Mr. Geiger had given her *was* pretty impressive.

Nina pushed aside a pile of wrapping paper and stood up.

"This is the part when we all join hands and dance around the Christmas tree. We sing 'O Come All Ye Faithful' and offer up gifts to Our Savior."

"Oh, my!" Sarah looked as if she were about to bolt toward the front door.

"That's my sister's twisted idea of a joke, Sarah," Claire said quickly.

"Claire's right. This is actually the part when we all pitch in and help you prepare the great Christmas dinner you promised."

The Geigers' housekeeper, Janelle, spent every Christmas with her daughter in Vermont. Nina, Claire, and Mr. Geiger usually just heated up TV dinners and made ice-cream sundaes. But Sarah had insisted on making a "real" Christmas dinner, despite the fact that she was Jewish.

"This is my first Christmas ever," Sarah chirped for the third time. "I feel like I'm five years old."

"So you're not, like, offended that we're celebrating the birth of Christ or anything?" Nina asked.

Mr. Geiger glared at his younger daughter. "Nina, that's enough."

Nina shrugged. "Since when is mentioning Jesus on Christmas a sin?"

143

"Come on, Nina," Claire said. "You're the one who's always harping about Christmas being a commercial holiday. You're about as religious as my elbow."

"I always enjoy experiencing new things," Aaron interjected diplomatically.

Nina flashed a bright smile, looking almost human. "Hey, who can say no to presents?"

Claire stared at Aaron, thinking of the framed map of the solar system he'd given her. He'd said that since she was always gazing at the sky, she might as well know what she was looking at. Claire had been speechless when she opened the gift.

She just hadn't been prepared to be so touched by the fact that he understood her well enough to buy the elusive perfect gift. In her opinion, it was another sign (not that she needed another) that they should be together.

Feeling dangerously close to bursting into happy tears, Claire stood. "I'm going to go get dressed," she announced.

As she walked from the living room, Claire felt Aaron's eyes on her. Her spine tingled. Maybe by the end of the day she and Aaron would have their own holiday celebration—in private.

Zoey stamped her feet hard on the Geigers' front porch as she waited for Nina to answer the door. She'd finally escaped the house by saying she had to take Nina her Christmas present. Which was almost true. She, Nina, and Aisha had agreed not to damage their bank accounts any more than they already had by exchanging gifts. But Zoey did have something for Aaron, who was at Nina's.

"Merry Christmas!" Nina cried. Then she looked disappointed. "Where's Benjamin?"

Zoey walked into the house and began unlacing her boots. "Nice to see you, too. He told me to tell you he'll be over later. For some reason he feels compelled to make Lara feel like an actual member of our family today."

"Well, I'm glad you're here. Sarah Sunshine is driving me insane."

"Aaron's here, isn't he?" Zoey whispered.

Nina rolled her eyes. "Yes, he's here. But Lucas is the one you're in love with. Remember?"

Zoey narrowed her eyes. "Lucas informed me that I made him sick, in case you'd forgotten." She'd already decided she wasn't going to give Lucas his Christmas present. Not until he begged her forgiveness for the scene he'd made at Aisha's.

Nina took Zoey's coat and draped it over a chair in the foyer. "He was upset. It's understandable."

"He *ruined* my Christmas."

"You're being totally unreasonable. You're the one who stuck a dagger in his heart by fooling around behind his back."

"Hey, I didn't do anything he didn't do."

"Zoey, you're not in love with Aaron. How could you be? The guy is a snake in hiding."

Zoey pulled off her second boot. "Nina, he's the sweetest guy on earth!"

Nina shrugged. "Benjamin and I were talking about it last night. We decided it's just an act."

"Well, I really don't care what—" Zoey's voice broke off as Aaron appeared behind Nina's back.

"Oh, Aaron, we were just talking about you," Nina said sweetly.

145

"Hi, Aaron." Zoey stared down at the gift in her hands, feeling embarrassed.

"I'll just go make sure Claire isn't slipping arsenic into the apple pie," Nina said.

When she was gone, Aaron reached out and squeezed Zoey's shoulder. "I'm really sorry about that scene at the party last night."

"Oh, yeah, well . . . Lucas was being a real jerk."

"I don't want to interfere, but maybe you *should* dump the guy. He seems a little unstable."

Zoey felt immediately defensive. She could say anything she wanted to about Lucas, but she didn't appreciate anyone else putting him down. Not even Aaron. "He was just upset," Zoey said, echoing Nina's words.

Aaron shrugged. "Whatever."

Zoey remembered her present. "I know you don't celebrate Christmas or anything, but I got you a little present anyway. I hope you don't mind." She held out the gift.

"Are you kidding? Of course I don't mind." He grinned. "I, uh, got something for you, too." He held out his left hand, which he'd been holding behind his back. "I was kind of hoping you'd stop by."

Zoey felt herself blush. "Oh, Aaron. You didn't have to."

"I wanted to, Zoey." He took the present she was holding and handed her the small package in his hands. "You first."

Zoey unwrapped the paper slowly. "A harmonica!"

He beamed. "Yeah. And there's a beginner's teaching guide, too."

"This is great. A hobby."

He looked into her eyes. "When you get good, we can play together."

Zoey laughed uneasily. "You'll probably be gone by then."

"Yeah. I guess I will be."

"Maybe I can made a recording and send it to you. . . ."

"Just think of me while you're playing. I'll be listening."

Zoey was starting to feel slightly dizzy. She'd planned on having a light, friendly conversation with Aaron, but there was more than friendship in the air. "Open yours," she said quickly.

He tore away the paper, revealing the songbook she'd gotten him. "Hey, we're on the same wavelength. It must be destiny."

Before Zoey could respond, Claire poked her head around the corner. "Hi, Zoey," she said unenthusiastically. "Aaron, we're ready to eat."

Claire disappeared, and Zoey began quickly pulling on her boots. Obviously the Geigers weren't interested in extra company. "I've gotta go," she said to Aaron.

"Thanks for the present, Zoey. It means a lot to me."

Zoey looked up from her boot laces. "Me too. About the harmonica, I mean." She stood up and pulled on her coat. "Well, Merry Christmas."

Aaron stepped close to her. "You're forgetting something."

"I am?" Zoey looked around the small foyer, then saw that Aaron was pointing to a spot over the door.

"Mistletoe," he whispered.

Aaron wrapped his arms around her waist and

slowly lowered his face toward hers. As Zoey met his lips she experienced several emotions. She felt excited by the kiss, as she had felt *every* time she kissed him. She also felt guilty for going behind Lucas's back yet again. Then she felt confused, because she realized that she and Lucas were more or less broken up and she didn't need to feel guilty anymore. The last sensation Zoey noted was nausea.

Kissing two different guys within twenty-four hours was *not* good for the digestive system.

Seventeen

Christmas night Jake sat on the floor of his bedroom, his back against the bed. In his lap he cradled the bottle of vodka he'd stolen from the Grays' house the night before.

Jake took a long swig from the bottle. He was far past the point of flinching at the bitter taste. He didn't even feel the liquid as it flowed down his throat.

He brushed a tear away from his cheek. He couldn't believe he was spending Christmas night alone. Lara had called at eight o'clock and canceled his plans with her in favor of playing Pictionary with the Passmores. She'd said she needed to make an effort to "do the family thing."

Jake laughed bitterly. Of course, *he* could "do the family thing," too. But that would involve watching his mother's sad face as she leafed through old family albums, as she had every Christmas since Wade's death. Jake shook his head. No way was he going to put himself through that misery. He was better off alone.

Jake swallowed another gulp of vodka, then tried to stand up. He decided to put on a little music. Some blues, maybe. He staggered toward his stereo, giggling. He was drunker than he'd thought. In fact, he was wasted. He looked down at the bottle. It was almost empty.

Trying to focus on the goal of reaching his stereo, Jake lurched forward. But when he reached for the power button, he misjudged the distance. Jake fell to the floor, the stereo crashing on top of him. The bottle slipped from his fingers and rolled across the floor. Jake lay on his back, laughing. So much for music.

Moments later he heard footsteps running toward his door. Jake pushed the stereo off his chest in a futile attempt to sit up. The door opened.

"Jake, are you all right?" Mr. McRoyan yelled.

"Great, Dad. Never been better." Jake concentrated on pulling himself up onto his bed, trying to appear normal.

"Cut the crap, Jake. You're drunk."

Jake finally succeeded in getting himself onto the bed. He giggled. "Come on, Dad. 'Tis the season to be jolly. So I've had a little eggnog. Big deal."

Mr. McRoyan's face had turned pale. He came farther into the room, slamming the door behind him. Through his drunken haze, Jake felt a wave of fear.

"Do you think I'm an idiot?" Mr. McRoyan shouted. "Do you think I don't know what goes on in my own house?"

"I don't know what you're talking about. . . ." Jake's voice trailed off as he saw his dad staring at the empty vodka bottle.

"Don't bother lying, Jake. I've noticed the twelve-packs disappearing from the garage." He picked up the bottle from the floor. "God only knows where you got this."

Jake waved his hands in the air. "Okay. You caught me. I've stolen a few cases of beer."

"And liquor, Jake. You've been pouring water into our liquor bottles to hide the fact that it's disappearing." Mr. McRoyan tossed the bottle into the trash can next to Jake's desk, an expression of pure disgust on his face. "I hadn't noticed until I poured myself a scotch the other night."

Jake forced himself to sit up straighter, although his stomach was churning and he felt slightly dizzy. "See, you drink. Why shouldn't I?"

"For one thing, you're underage. Several years underage."

"Wade drank," Jake said quietly. "He drank a lot."

Mr. McRoyan's face got even whiter. "And look where it got him. He's six feet underground, and the rest of us are left trying to pick up the pieces."

"Dad!" Jake felt tears rise to the surface. He was a failure. A total, complete, one hundred percent failure as a son.

When Mr. McRoyan spoke again, his voice was heavy with emotion. "Jake, I don't want that to happen to you. I don't think I could stand it. I don't think your mother could stand it." He sat down next to Jake on the bed, his head in his hands.

"Don't pretend that you care about her, Dad," Jake said, his voice accusing. "You're screwing every woman you can get your hands on."

"Shut up!" Mr. McRoyan yelled. Jake had never seen him so angry.

Jake closed his eyes, miserable. "Hey, I'm just stating the facts. Don't shoot the messenger."

"I love your mother. Very much. I'm not excusing what I've done, but I want you to know that she

151

means everything to me." His voice was low and serious but calmer.

"You've sure got a funny way of showing it."

"And your way is better, I suppose?"

"I've never done anything to Mom."

Mr. McRoyan stood up and grabbed Jake by the arm. He pulled him roughly off the bed and dragged him into the bathroom. Jake saw his own pathetic reflection in the mirror.

"Look at yourself. You don't think it would hurt your mom to walk in here and find you like this?"

Jake looked into his bloodshot eyes. His shirt was splattered with vodka, and there was a cut on his cheek from where the edge of the stereo had hit him. Across his forehead was a shiny layer of perspiration.

Suddenly the fight left him. He couldn't struggle anymore. It was just too hard. Jake collapsed against his father's strong chest, tears flowing freely down his cheek. "I tried to stop, Dad."

Mr. McRoyan put his arms around him, hugging him close. "I know, son. I know."

"I don't want to be this way."

Mr. McRoyan moved Jake's head so that he could look into his eyes. "I'm going to help you," he said fiercely. "I'm not going to let you slip away, the way I did with Wade."

Jake allowed his father to lead him back into the bedroom, where Mr. McRoyan pushed him gently into bed. As he lay down, Jake felt truly peaceful for the first time in months, if not years. His dad was there for him. He was going to help him make things better.

"I love you, Dad," Jake said quietly.

"I love you, too." Mr. McRoyan switched off the

light next to Jake's bed. "Now get some sleep. We're taking you to an AA meeting first thing in the morning."

"Today was really great, Eesh," Christopher said.

"Yeah, I love Christmas."

Christopher and Aisha were sitting on the Grays' living room couch. Everyone else was already in bed, and they'd turned off all the lights but those on the Christmas tree.

"I mean, spending the day with your family. It meant a lot to me."

Aisha snuggled closer against Christopher's chest. "It meant a lot to me, too, Christopher."

He sighed, running his fingers through her hair. "I never had a Christmas like this. My mom just wasn't into it."

Aisha took Christopher's hand and traced the lines of his palm with her thumb. She felt an over-powering wave of love for her boyfriend. He'd already been through so much. His family was totally dysfunctional, and he'd made the decision to separate himself from them so he could make a better life for himself. But she knew he was often lonely.

"You deserve a Norman Rockwell Christmas every year from now on," she said.

"This is what I want, Aisha. A great family, a nice home. Presents under the tree."

"You'll get it. I know you will."

His arm tightened around her. "I want it with *you*, Eesh."

As Aisha stared at the tree, its lights blurred. She pictured herself twenty years in the future, sitting with Christopher on Christmas night. Their kids would be safe in bed, and then they'd sit together on the couch, laughing and kissing. Later they would make beautiful love in their king-sized bed.

"What are you thinking?" Christopher asked.

She shook her head. "Nothing."

"Was it about me?"

"Yeah."

"Was it about saying yes to marrying me?"

She nodded, then turned to look at him. She couldn't put off giving him an answer forever, but she couldn't say yes just then. Not when her head was filled with fantasies that might never come true. Because marrying Christopher wasn't just about Christmas night and lights and presents. It was about a lifelong commitment—one she wasn't sure she could make.

"New Year's Eve," she said.

"What about it?"

"I'll give you an answer by midnight on New Year's Eve. I promise."

Six days. She had six days in which to make a decision that was going to affect the rest of her life.

Eighteen

"Well, I guess this is it," Benjamin said Thursday afternoon.

Zoey felt a tear slide down her cheek. "Good luck, Benjamin." Her voice broke, and she hugged him close.

"Hey, no crying. You'll make me feel guilty if the operation is a failure."

"It's going to be a success," Zoey said adamantly. "I can feel it."

"Of course it will be," Mrs. Passmore said.

Mr. Passmore threw a duffel bag over his shoulder. "Zo, are you sure you can manage the restaurant on your own?"

"Yes, Dad," she said for the fifth time that day.

He patted her on the shoulder. "Well, Lara's going to be here."

Zoey tried to smile. "That's a big comfort."

"And Christopher's coming in at six. You just have to get there by five to set up for dinner. No lunch today."

"Dad, she knows," Benjamin said.

"Okay, okay. Just checking."

Mrs. Passmore pulled on her husband's arm. "We've got to go, Jeff."

"Yeah. Nina's probably already at the ferry, wondering if I've changed my mind," Benjamin said.

Zoey hugged Benjamin one last time. "I'm sorry I can't be with you."

"You're better off here, trust me. Besides, what're we going to do? Hand the restaurant over to Lara?"

"Ugh, don't remind me."

"Bye, Zo."

"Good-bye, Benjamin."

Zoey watched as her family headed down the block, each carrying a duffel bag. Benjamin looked cool and confident, but Zoey knew he must be terrified.

She wished there were something she could do for him. Ever since Benjamin had become blind, Zoey had tried to protect him. For his sake, she always tried to pretend that he didn't need any special help. Benjamin hated to be coddled. But he *was* different, and he did need help—occasionally.

She just hoped he had the strength to deal with the outcome of the surgery. Because just as there was a fifty percent chance that he *would* see again . . . there was just as good a chance that he wouldn't.

A little after five that afternoon Zoey walked around Passmores', setting out forks and napkins on each of the empty tables. Lara was sitting behind the cash register, looking bored.

"Want to help me with this?" Zoey asked.

"Actually, I was thinking about making popcorn," she responded.

Zoey glanced up. "Popcorn?"

"Yeah. You know, the fluffy white stuff people eat at the movies? I saw a jar in the kitchen and got a craving."

Zoey reminded herself that her mother had given her specific instructions to be nice to Lara. "Well, uh, I don't think we actually have a popper here."

Lara shrugged. "No prob. I'll cook it in oil. I used to do it all the time."

"I don't know . . . maybe you should wait for Christopher."

Lara laughed. "Jeez, it's just some stupid popcorn. Chill out."

Zoey rammed a fork into her palm to keep from saying something rude. "Fine. Suit yourself."

Lara disappeared into the kitchen. Zoey continued to set the tables, forcing herself to take deep, even breaths. She'd read once that good breathing could keep a person from losing her temper.

After a couple of minutes Lara emerged from the kitchen. "Now I just have to wait for the oil to heat up."

"Fascinating," Zoey said. She grabbed a handful of knives from the flatware bin. What she wouldn't give to stick one straight into Lara's back.

Lara picked up some spoons. "I'll help."

"Gee, thanks."

Lara followed Zoey, putting down a spoon next to each of the knives. "So, what's up with you and Lucas?" Lara asked suddenly.

Zoey flinched. Great. Now the girl wanted to have a tête-à-tête. "Nothing."

"Are you guys, like, back together?"

Zoey stopped in her tracks. Lara had never shown any interest in her relationship with Lucas before. She'd only asked about Jake. A horrifying thought popped into Zoey's head. "Why? Do you want him for yourself?"

Lara glared at her. "What's that supposed to mean?"

"Come on, Lara. You took my old boyfriend, not to mention my dad. Why wouldn't you want another one of the men in my life?"

"You're a pathetic little brat," Lara said coldly. "Perfect little Zoey, everybody's darling. You've got everyone believing you're an angel. But you are *far* from an angel. You don't even deserve a guy like Lucas—"

"Do you smell something?" Zoey interrupted. She'd been so furious with Lara and her little speech that she hadn't noticed at first, but there was the distinct smell of something burning in the kitchen. Something like a pan of oil.

"Uh-oh." Lara let her spoons clatter to the floor and raced to the kitchen. Zoey was close behind.

"Oh, my God!" Zoey screamed when she reached the door of the kitchen.

Lara's popcorn oil was on fire. The room was filled with dense smoke, and flames were shooting up over the stove. It looked as if the whole thing was going to blow.

"Damn," Lara muttered.

Zoey ran to the telephone, frantically trying to remember the phone number of someone who belonged to the volunteer fire department. But her mind was blank.

Finally she picked up the phone and dialed. On the second ring he picked up.

"Lucas!" she yelled. "Get down to Passmores' now! I need you!"

She slammed down the phone, then ran toward the kitchen. As she walked through clouds of smoke toward the fire extinguisher, she prayed that Lucas would get there soon.

Six hours later Lucas sat in his bedroom, staring at the small box that contained Zoey's gift. Despite the fact that he had absolutely no intention of giving her the present, he'd spent forty-five minutes painstakingly wrapping the stupid thing. He'd even had his mom show him how to make a perfect bow.

Claire had told him that Zoey had gotten him a gift, too. She must have still cared about him a little, he reasoned. No one went out and bought a present for someone they weren't at least a little bit in love with. Did they?

Lucas sighed heavily. Why hadn't he just gone over to her house the day before? He could have knocked on the door, handed Zoey the present, then split. No big emotional scene, no yelling. Just a simple delivery of a holiday gift.

Lucas grabbed the present and shoved it under his pillow. He knew why he hadn't gone to the Passmores' on Christmas—because Zoey had made a total scene at Aisha's party by flirting with Aaron. Well, maybe she hadn't technically been flirting, but she'd been friendly. No jury would find otherwise.

But she hadn't called Aaron when she'd really needed help that afternoon at the restaurant. She'd called Lucas. Lucas was the one she trusted. He was the one she loved.

By the time Lucas had arrived at the restaurant, Zoey had put the fire out with the extinguisher. When he'd come into the kitchen, she'd been standing in the middle of the still smoky room, staring at the ruins of the stove.

"Thanks for coming, but it's over," she'd said in a daze.

It would have been easy for him to go give her a hug. To offer to help clean up the mess. But instead Lucas had headed straight for the door. "I guess you don't need me after all," he'd said.

Zoey hadn't responded. She'd just gazed around the kitchen, looking crushed.

Now Lucas jumped when he heard a knock on the door. "Lucas someone's here to see you," his mother called softly. "Although I must say, it's awfully late."

His heart raced, and he felt his palms sweat. Finally Zoey had come. He felt like dancing a jig in the middle of his room. She loved him.

He'd sensed it at the restaurant that afternoon, but he hadn't allowed himself to hope. He'd tried to close off his emotions behind a mental iron curtain. And now she was there.

"Hi, Lucas."

His heart sank to somewhere just below his toes. It wasn't Zoey. Sure, she had Zoey's cornflower blue eyes. She was even wearing a very Zoey-like white blouse. But she was most definitely not the girl he loved.

"Uh, hi, Lara," he said.

"I just, um, wanted to get some advice about Zoey," she said, walking into the room. "She's totally pissed off at me after the, uh, kitchen accident. She won't even speak to me. I thought you might have some tips on how I could get along with her better."

Lara smiled sweetly and sank down next to him on the bed. Lucas stared at her in disbelief. Did the girl live on Mars? He couldn't believe she was coming to *him* about how to get along with Zoey. The irony was so bitter, he almost laughed.

Lucas tried to smile at Lara, who seemed to be giving him an intense once-over with her wide blue eyes. But he couldn't quite manage to lift the corners of his mouth. All he wanted to do was go off and find a nice, peaceful place to die.

Nineteen

Nina tiptoed into room 414, still tingling from Benjamin's good-night kiss. Kisses. Mrs. Passmore had already turned out the lamp, and the heavy motel curtains (they resembled hanging bedspreads) blocked out the lights from outside.

She made her way carefully to the bathroom, hoping not to wake Benjamin's mom. Halfway there, the sharp edge of a large object came into contact with her kneecap. She grunted softly.

"Don't worry about the noise, Nina. I'm still awake." The light was switched on suddenly, and Nina realized she'd walked directly into the TV set.

"Oh, hi, Mrs. P. I'm just going to change." Nina grabbed her duffel bag from the floor and sprinted toward the bathroom. "You can turn off the light now."

In the fluorescent light of the bathroom, Nina studied her face. She was glad Benjamin hadn't been able to see the dark circles under her eyes or the worried frown lines she seemed to have developed overnight.

Nina slipped into her new flannel pajamas, then decided against brushing her teeth. She was too preoccupied to concentrate on the state of her gums.

She switched off the light, then felt her way (more carefully this time) to her bed.

Nina slipped under the covers, wishing Benjamin were there to share the queen-sized mattress. She knew instantly that the odds of falling asleep were about equal to the chances of her winning the lottery. She closed her eyes anyway. Maybe if she faked sleep, she'd feel rested by morning.

Minutes passed. Nina listened to the ticking of Mrs. Passmore's travel alarm clock, trying to count each minute as it passed.

"Nina?" Mrs. Passmore called softly in the darkness.

Damn, Nina thought. She'd been hoping to avoid pillow talk with Mrs. Passmore.

"Yeah, Mrs. P.?"

"I couldn't help overhearing part of the conversation you girls were having the other night."

Nina's heart stopped. This was a nightmare. Nina pinched herself. She would wake up any second now. She had to. Several moments went by, in which Nina realized that this was *not* a nightmare.

Her boyfriend's mother actually wanted to talk to her about sex. And Nina was trapped in the small confines of this dreary room in the Malibu Hotel. She waited for a natural disaster. Why weren't there ever earthquakes in Boston? Or tornadoes? Even a small hurricane would do the trick.

"Nina? Did you hear me?"

Nina felt blood rush to her cheeks. She was glad that at least the room was dark, so Mrs. Passmore couldn't see her face turning the color of an over-cooked lobster. She briefly considered playing dumb, then decided that could make the situation even more humiliating.

"Oh, yeah. Well."

She heard Mrs. Passmore turning over in bed. "I don't want to embarrass you. Really."

Nina threw the scratchy hotel blanket over her face. "I appreciate that, but I think it's kind of too late."

Unfortunately, Mrs. Passmore sounded unfazed. "In that case, I might as well go on with my little speech."

"Oh, I really don't think that's necessary, Mrs. P." Silently Nina cursed Zoey and her stupid slumber party.

"If your own mother were still alive, I'd agree with you." Her voice was kind but firm.

"Is it my imagination, or did I hear a *but* at the end of that sentence?" Nina asked.

Mrs. Passmore laughed. "I know how much you girls hate talking about sex with us old folks, *but* we're just trying to make things easier for you."

Nina considered her options. She could offer as little information as possible and hope that Mrs. Passmore would take mercy on her and shut up. Or she could come right out and tell the woman the answer to the question she was doubtlessly leading up to, thereby avoiding unnecessary sex chat. Nina decided to go for ending the torture quickly.

"Weusedacondom," she said in one long exhalation.

"Sorry, I didn't understand you." Now that her eyes were fully adjusted to the darkness, Nina could see that Mrs. Passmore was propped up on one elbow, leaning forward slightly to hear her words.

Nina rolled her eyes. The most humiliating moment of her life, take two. "I said, we used a condom."

Mrs. Passmore lay back down. "Well, I'm glad to hear it."

"These days they teach us all about safe sex in school. It's not like when you were young—"

Nina bit her tongue. On top of everything else, she'd violated rule number twenty-seven: Never remind a middle-aged person that they were past their peak.

Luckily, Mrs. Passmore laughed. "I'm not that old, Nina. Believe it or not, I've even had sex a few times."

"Uh, Mrs. P.?" she croaked.

"Yeah?"

"Could we just, like, go to sleep now?"

Again Mrs. Passmore laughed quietly. "Good night, Nina."

" 'Night." Nina rolled over and attempted to suffocate herself with her pillow.

When after two minutes she was still alive, Nina curled into a fetal position. As she stared at the dark wall, a strange sensation washed over her.

She'd kind of liked talking to Mrs. Passmore about sex. For a few minutes she'd actually felt as if she still had a mother. A tear rolled down Nina's cheek as she wondered what kind of lecture her own mom would have given her about sex. Or about anything else, for that matter.

"Hey, Nina?" Mrs. Passmore said suddenly.

"Yeah?"

"Benjamin's going to be okay. Whichever way the surgery goes, he'll be okay."

Nina closed her eyes. At last she felt close to being sleepy. In her half-conscious haze, Nina hoped Zoey and Benjamin realized how lucky they were.

A nice set of parents was pretty handy to have around. Sometimes.

Next door, in room 416 of the Malibu Hotel, Benjamin was wide awake. He wished he'd brought his Braille clock. He had no idea if he'd been lying in bed for five minutes or five hours.

"Are you awake, Dad?" he whispered.

"Yeah."

"Me too."

"I doubt you'll get much sleep tonight, Benjamin. You've got a big day tomorrow."

Benjamin sat up a little, leaning against the bed's thin wood headboard. "I feel like tonight is a combination of Christmas Eve, when I still believed in Santa Claus, and the night before I went in to get a root canal."

Benjamin heard his dad roll over. "To tell you the truth, the same thing's going on with me. I can't remember the last time I felt so keyed up."

"I'm really scared, Dad." Benjamin hoped his father didn't notice just how shaky his voice was.

"I know." Mr. Passmore sighed. "I wish I could take you on my lap and tell you everything was going to be okay, the way I did when you were little. . . ."

"But?" Benjamin asked.

"But you're not little anymore, Benjamin. And I don't have all the answers. I don't even have most of the answers."

Benjamin reached for his Ray-Bans, which he'd put close to him on the bedside table. He felt suddenly that he needed all the comfort he could get. Some people had teddy bears. He had sunglasses.

"Am I crazy to be putting myself through this,

Dad?'' he asked. "I mean, I'm used to being blind. I don't even think about it half the time.''

"Benjamin, you'd be crazy *not* to take this chance. We never know what life is going to throw in our direction. But we can't run away from the surprises.''

"Sort of like you and Lara, I guess.''

"Exactly.''

"I just hope I'm strong enough to deal with this.''

"We all love you, Benjamin. No matter what happens, we're going to be there for you, every step of the way.'' Mr. Passmore's voice broke, then he coughed.

"Thanks, but I think this is a solo mission.'' Benjamin imagined his dad nodding, his long gray ponytail bobbing up and down.

"Unfortunately, the big things often are.''

Benjamin slid down until his head hit the flat pillow. "Good night, Dad.''

"Sweet dreams, Benjamin.''

Twenty

Zoey stood in the Passmores' kitchen, glad to be out of the restaurant. She'd put a Closed sign on the restaurant door, then she and Christopher had spent hours cleaning up the mess from the fire extinguisher and the fire. Lara had conveniently disappeared as soon as the crisis was over.

Zoey gazed at Lucas's house as she rubbed a towel through her damp hair. She'd spent half an hour in the shower, but she still reeked of smoke and burnt oil.

Lucas's light was on, although the rest of the Cabrals' house was dark. She imagined him sitting on his bed, possibly even thinking about her.

Zoey sat down at the kitchen table and stared at the small wrapped package in front of her. She'd taken Lucas's Christmas present out from under her bed and brought it downstairs with her. Why?

She ran her finger over the gift's silver bow, then glanced back up at Lucas's window. She hadn't even told him what was wrong when she'd called from the restaurant, but he'd come. He'd been panting when he'd come into the kitchen. Judging from how quickly he'd arrived, Zoey knew he must have sprinted all the way from his house to the restaurant. As she'd known he would.

She thought back to that terrible moment. The kitchen had been on fire; she'd been panicked. The idea of calling Aaron had never entered her mind. And the whole time she'd been desperately spraying the fire extinguisher, she hadn't thought of Aaron.

She'd wanted only Lucas, the guy she was in love with. If only she'd reached out to him or he'd reached out to her. But she hadn't. And he hadn't. So he'd left.

Zoey picked up the present. This was stupid and needless. She belonged with Lucas, and he belonged with her. Any moron could see that.

She didn't bother putting on her coat. Her adrenaline was pumping so hard that she could have gone out in a blizzard and not felt the cold.

Zoey ran out the front door carrying the gift. Her spirits soared. She was on her way to Lucas. In just minutes they would be together.

She jogged to the back of the house, then quickly climbed the dirt path that led to the Cabrals'. As she went she thought of the dozens of times she'd met Lucas at this same spot, giggling—clandestine meetings for a last kiss before bed.

At the Cabrals' front door, she hesitated. Mr. Cabral went to bed while most people were still watching the evening news, and Mrs. Cabral usually wasn't too far behind. Ringing the bell was out of the question.

Zoey decided to take a chance on the door being unlocked. If it wasn't, she'd have to throw pebbles at Lucas's window until she got his attention. Luck was on her side. The door opened easily, and Zoey crept inside.

She moved quietly through the dark house, her excitement mounting. With every step she was closer to Lucas.

At last she reached his door. Without knocking, she flung it open. Beaming, she entered the room.

"Lucas, I love you," she announced. And then her heart stopped.

He wasn't alone. Sitting right next to him on the bed was Lara. Wearing the blouse Zoey had bought her for Christmas, she was practically sitting in Lucas's lap.

"Zoey!" Lucas cried, standing up.

Using sheer force of will, Zoey kept herself from fainting. She turned first to Lara. "You're a slut," she said quietly.

"Zoey, it's not like that—" Lucas began.

She moved her dangerously cold stare to his pale face. "And you're a bastard." Zoey threw the carefully wrapped box at Lucas's head. "Merry Christmas."

Leaving Lucas stammering mindlessly behind her, Zoey fled.

Claire approached Gray House from the side, shuffling through the grass so that inquiring eyes wouldn't notice any distinct footprints in the snow. The night was pitch-black, and the air smelled crisp and sharp. With any luck, there would be more snow.

Claire inhaled deeply, enjoying the cold sting of wind on her cheeks. She knelt down to the right of the Grays' front porch, then tugged off one glove with her teeth. She moved her hand through the thin layer of snow that covered the ground, searching for the small red brick she knew lay in the vicinity.

After several seconds, Claire closed her fingers around the ice-cold brick. Success. She'd seen Aisha retrieve the front door key from this hiding place on a few occasions over the past couple of years, but she'd never guessed how valuable this particular information would become.

Claire closed her eyes for a moment, willing the key to be there. She picked up the brick and felt around on the ground beneath it. Nothing. Claire cursed softly. Then she turned the brick over in her hand and smiled. The key was frozen to the bottom. Claire unstuck the object of her search, then crept onto the front porch. Her ability to move silently would make or break her mission.

The key fit easily into the lock, and slowly she opened the door. The hinges squeaked, and she froze. But when she heard no footsteps, Claire continued into the house.

She shut the door gently behind her, then slipped off the loafers she'd worn expressly because they were easy to remove. With her shoes dangling from one hand, Claire tiptoed toward the staircase.

This was it. Either the best or the worst moment of her life was about to occur. In just seconds she'd be in Aaron's bedroom, where he was no doubt sleeping peacefully.

As she climbed the stairs Claire felt almost eerily calm. It was as if every event of her life had been building up to this single, daring move. She didn't care that Aaron had given Zoey a dumb harmonica for Christmas or that she'd seen them kissing under the mistletoe. Those had been only minor setbacks.

Because she was sure that Aaron was just using Zoey. Claire thought of the last time she'd sneaked into Aaron's room. She'd found a letter from some totally naive girl who'd believed that Aaron was in love with her just because she'd stupidly had sex with him. A girl who was probably very similar to Zoey. Sweet. Naive. Trusting.

But Claire was a woman. A woman who would appreciate the *real* Aaron—not the cardboard cutout he put on for show. With increasing confidence, she padded softly to his door.

She stopped in front of his room, forcing herself to rein in her mounting excitement. There was still one more possible obstacle. She was taking a chance that Aaron hadn't locked his door. Claire turned the knob slowly, then breathed a sigh of relief when the door opened. She was in.

The room was almost pitch-black. Claire closed the door behind her, then stood still to wait for her eyes to adjust to the darkness. From the bed, she heard Aaron's deep, even breathing.

After a couple of minutes Claire bent down and placed her loafers on the small throw rug next to the door. Then she moved purposefully toward Aaron's bed.

He was on his stomach, sprawled diagonally across the mattress. She longed to reach out and stroke the dark curls of his hair, which stood out in high relief against the white of his pillowcase. *Easy, girl*, she cautioned herself. Any sudden movements would spoil the effect of her performance.

Claire continued to stare. Sheets and blankets were tangled around Aaron's legs as if he'd been at war with the bedclothes. She took a sharp breath as she realized that Aaron was wearing nothing but a loose pair of boxers.

Claire bit her lip, feeling uncertain for the first

time since she'd crept out of her house almost half an hour earlier. Was she insane? Had she gone completely over the *Fatal Attraction* edge? Claire Geiger wasn't used to throwing herself at *anybody*. But Aaron wasn't anybody. He was the guy that God—if there was one—had custom-designed for her benefit.

She picked up the edge of the sheet that hung over the side of the bed. Then, taking a deep, steadying breath, Claire climbed into bed with Aaron Mendel.

As her full weight dented the mattress, Aaron stirred. Claire slid closer to him, reaching out at last to touch his perfect hair. When he felt her hand moving gently over his head, Aaron groaned in his sleep. Claire inched even closer.

Carefully she touched her lips to his. As she'd expected, they were both soft and firm. Her body tingled as she felt him return the pressure.

Claire watched as Aaron's eyes fluttered open. Quickly she reached out and covered his eyes with her hand. "Just kiss me," she whispered.

Still only half awake, he pulled her close, then captured her lips in the most incredible kiss Claire had ever experienced.

Suddenly Claire realized that although his eyes were closed, Aaron was now fully awake. His hands moved up and down her sides, sending shivers across her entire body.

"Zoey . . . ," he murmured, holding her even more tightly.

Claire stiffened. "It's not Zoey," she whispered. Aaron's hazel eyes opened. He stared at Claire, penetrating her with his gaze. "Sorry to disappoint you."

He brought his mouth just millimeters from hers.

She saw that he was smiling. "Hello, Claire. Fancy meeting you here."

She smiled back. "I just happened to be in the neighborhood. . . ."

Twenty-one

In Benjamin's dream, two weeks had passed. He was ready to take off his bandages, and for the big event, his parents, Zoey, and Nina drove him out to the country. They led him into deep woods, then spun him around and around until he fell from dizziness. Finally, with a triumphant cry, he tore the cloth from his eyes. And saw nothing.

Moments later, there was the sound of footsteps. People running through the forests, stepping on twigs in their haste.

"Don't leave me!" Benjamin screamed. "Nina, come back! Zoey!"

But there were no voices. Just the chirping of birds and the sharp hiss of a snake. Benjamin was alone. Utterly, dreadfully alone.

Now Benjamin put a hand over his pounding heart. He was drenched in sweat; a drop trickled from his hairline down his cheek.

"Dad!" he yelled.

He heard his father hurrying to the bed. "Benjamin, what's wrong?"

"Nothing. Nothing. I, uh, guess I had a nightmare."

Benjamin felt his father brush his hand across the

top of his head. "I saw you tossing and turning, but I thought I'd let you sleep as long as possible."

"Well, I'm just as glad to be awake."

"Rise and shine, then. Let's get you to that hospital."

Benjamin took deep breaths, willing his heart to slow down. Everything's going to be fine, he told himself. When he took the bandages off, he'd be able to see. Maybe.

Nina sat in the back of the Passmores' van, wishing someone would say something. Anything. So far, the ride to Boston General had been about as cheerful as her mother's funeral.

"Wow!" she said brightly. "Usually I spend Christmas break just, like, catching up on the CBS soaps and arguing with Claire. This is much more exciting."

Benjamin pointed his Ray-Bans in her direction. "Yeah, it's a thrill a minute. We should do this *every* Christmas break."

"We're, uh, almost there," Mr. Passmore called back. Nina saw him eye Benjamin in the rearview mirror.

"Great, Dad. Can't wait." Benjamin moved closer to Nina.

She clutched his hand between both of hers. At moments like this, she wished she believed in vibes. If she did, she could send Benjamin a million positive vibrations, enough to carry him all the way through the experimental surgery.

Nina tried again. "While you're in surgery, I'll load up on candy bars from the vending machine. That way I'll have plenty of energy to entertain you when you wake up."

Benjamin leaned over and gave her a kiss on her cheek. "Just be there."

"I will be."

"Hey, I just thought of something," Benjamin said.

"What?" Mrs. Passmore asked.

"Maybe the surgery will reverse my blindness, but I'll wake up deaf."

Everyone was quiet. Nina stared at Benjamin in horror. He smiled, and Nina laughed. A joke. Finally, a joke.

"Or maybe you won't be able to feel or smell."

"Or taste," he added.

Nina giggled. "You could end up paralyzed."

"Maybe they'll accidentally amputate my arms and legs."

By now both Nina and Benjamin were laughing hysterically. The nervous tension Nina had been suppressing for the last several days burst out in the form of uncontrollable giggling. Beside her, Benjamin was shaking with silent laughter.

"You could become a vegetable!" Nina yelled.

"I always thought it would nice to be an artichoke."

"Or a piece of broccoli. Broccolis are very healthy."

"You two are sick," Mr. Passmore said sternly. But Nina saw that he was smiling.

"Really, your sense of humor is totally perverse," Mrs. Passmore added. "Not to mention entirely inappropriate."

Then Nina heard Mrs. Passmore laugh. Actually, it was more of a snort combined with a cough. Mr. Passmore followed suit.

Boston General's huge white building came into

view. By the time Mr. Passmore pulled into the parking lot, he and his three passengers were laughing wildly.

Nina took a deep breath. Everything was going to turn out great. As long as they kept laughing, nothing bad could happen.

Benjamin was lying on what he assumed was a hospital gurney. His clothes and sunglasses had been taken away; he was now wearing nothing but a very revealing hospital gown (he could feel the foot-wide gap in the back). Over his head were the voices of several nurses and a couple of doctors.

"How're you feeling, Benjamin?" Dr. Martin's voice was cheerful and booming.

"Fine, I guess. Sort of disoriented."

"You're in pre-op," Dr. Martin explained. "We're just about ready to hit the operating room and see what we can do for those eyes of yours."

"The sooner the better," Benjamin responded, although he was wondering if anyone would try to stop him if he jumped off the gurney and ran.

"Great, great." Benjamin heard approaching footsteps, then a whispered exchange between Dr. Martin and a female.

"What's going on?" Benjamin asked. "Is there some kind of problem?"

Dr. Martin chuckled. "Not unless you consider your girlfriend a problem. She wants a few words with you before we go into surgery."

A moment later Benjamin heard the unmistakable sound of Nina's Doc Martens stomping across the floor.

"You again," he said.

Nina took his hand, running her thumb back and

forth across his palm. "Show time," she said.

"Is that all you can say?"

He felt her hair brush his cheek, then her soft voice at his ear. "I'll be waiting for you."

"With candy bars?"

She laughed. "Twix. Baby Ruth. Snickers. Name your pleasure, sir."

"How about Milk Duds? I'll probably be feeling pretty dudlike when I wake up."

"Milk Duds it is. And Hershey's Kisses."

Benjamin groaned. "Don't get cheesy on me. Not when I need you at your most sarcastic."

"Okay. Scratch the Kisses."

"I love you, Nina."

She squeezed his shoulder. "I think the anesthesia's going to your head."

"They haven't given me any yet."

"Oh." He heard her voice tremble. He could always tell when Nina was holding back tears.

"Okay, kids, time to go," Dr. Martin said suddenly. Benjamin had forgotten he was there.

The gurney began to move, and Nina's hand slipped from his. "Aren't you going to say it back?" he called to her.

"I love you, Benjamin," she yelled.

The doctors and nurses laughed as they continued to move the gurney. A few minutes later the gurney stopped. Benjamin took a deep breath. He knew they were in the operating room. He could smell disinfectant and felt a rubber-gloved hand brush his hair away from his forehead.

"Okay, Benjamin. We're ready to start." Dr. Martin's voice was suddenly serious.

"You're sure everything is sterilized?" Benjamin joked feebly.

"Positive."

Benjamin's heart raced. "Okay, then."

"You're going to feel a little prick," Dr. Martin informed him pleasantly.

A second later Benjamin felt a needle being stuck into the back of his hand. He bit the inside of his cheek to keep from crying out.

"Now, start counting backward from one hundred," Dr. Martin told him.

Panic set in. They were going to operate while he was conscious. He would move his head and the knife would gouge out his entire eyeball. He was never going to be able to see again. Never.

"I don't feel sleepy at all, Dr. Martin," he said quickly. "This stuff isn't working."

"Calm down, Benjamin. Everything's fine. Just start counting."

Benjamin took a deep breath. He'd come too far to ruin it by having a mental breakdown. "One hundred, ninety-nine, ninety-eight, ninety-seven, ninety . . ."

Benjamin couldn't speak any longer. His entire body felt numb. As his eyes fluttered shut, Benjamin felt the onset of deep, deep sleep.

The last thing Benjamin heard, from what seemed like a million miles away, was the faint voice of Dr. Martin. "All right, team. Let's give this kid a miracle."

CALLING ALL TEEN READERS:

Do you like to read great books
featuring characters you can relate to?

Do you have strong opinions and lots of ideas
about books and reading?

Want to get free books, sneak previews,
and other stuff?

SEND FOR A FREE SAMPLER OF SOME OF THE GREATEST
TEEN FICTION BEING PUBLISHED NOW AND FIND OUT HOW YOU
CAN JOIN THE AVON TEMPEST FORECAST PROGRAM!

AVON TEMPEST IS A BRAND NEW PUBLISHING PROGRAM ESPECIALLY FOR
TEEN READERS, FEATURING CHARACTERS AND SITUATIONS YOU CAN RELATE
TO. RETURN THE COUPON BELOW, AND FOR YOUR TROUBLE WE'LL SEND
YOU A SAMPLER FEATURING EXCERPTS FROM FOUR GREAT BRAND NEW
AVON TEMPEST BOOKS, INCLUDING <u>SMACK</u> BY MELVIN BURGESS, <u>LITTLE
JORDAN</u> BY MARLY YOUMANS, <u>ANOTHER KIND OF MONDAY</u> BY WILLIAM
COLES AND <u>FADE FAR AWAY</u> BY FRANCESS LANTZ—PLUS INFORMATION
ON HOW YOU CAN JOIN THE AVON TEMPEST FORECAST PROGRAM TO GET
NEWS OF WHAT'S NEW AT AVON TEMPEST AND MORE FREE READING,
PLUS A CHANCE TO GIVE US YOUR IDEAS AND FEEDBACK ABOUT WHAT WE'RE
DOING.

AVON
tempest

✂ •

MAIL TO: AVON TEMPEST BOOKS, FORECAST PROGRAM, P.O. BOX
767, DRESDEN, TN 38225

☐ YES, I WANT TO SAMPLE SOME GREAT AVON TEMPEST FICTION AND
FIND OUT HOW TO JOIN THE AVON TEMPEST FORECAST PROGRAM.

name_____age____

address_____

city_____state____zip_____

e-mail (optional)_____

Making Out:
Claire Can't Lose

Book 12 in the explosive series about broken hearts, secrets, friendship, and of course, love.

Zoey still can't choose between **Aaron** and **Lucas,** so **Aaron** asks **Claire's** advice on how to win **Zoey's** heart for good. But **Claire** wants **Aaron** for herself. If he's crazy enough to follow her advice then...

Claire, can't lose

GET READY FOR THE STORM...

AVONtempest

PRESENTS CONTEMPORARY FICTION
FOR TEENS

SMACK
by Melvin Burgess
73223-8/$6.99 US

LITTLE JORDAN
by Marly Youmans
73136-3/$6.99 US/$8.99 Can

ANOTHER KIND OF MONDAY
by William E. Coles Jr.
73133-9/$6.99 US/$8.99 Can

FADE FAR AWAY
by Francess Lantz
79372-5/$6.99 US/$8.99 Can

3NBS OF JULIAN DREW
by James M. Deem
72587-3/$6.99 US/$8.99 Can